FINDING LOST

Also by Holly Goldberg Sloan

Keeper

I'll Be There

Counting by 7s

Just Call My Name

Appleblossom the Possum

Short

To Night Owl From Dogfish (with Meg Wolitzer)

The Elephant in the Room

Pieces of Blue

FINDING LOST

HOLLY GOLDBERG SLOAN

Rocky Pond Books

ROCKY POND BOOKS
An imprint of Penguin Random House LLC
1745 Broadway, New York, New York 10019

First published in the United States of America by Rocky Pond Books,
an imprint of Penguin Random House LLC, 2025

Copyright © 2025 by Holly Goldberg Sloan

Penguin Random House values and supports copyright.
Copyright fuels creativity, encourages diverse voices, promotes free
speech, and creates a vibrant culture. Thank you for buying an authorized edition
of this book and for complying with copyright laws by not reproducing, scanning, or
distributing any part of it in any form without permission. You are supporting writers
and allowing Penguin Random House to continue to publish books for every reader.
Please note that no part of this book may be used or reproduced in any manner
for the purpose of training artificial intelligence technologies or systems.

Rocky Pond Books and the Rocky Pond Books colophon
are registered trademarks of Penguin Random House LLC.

Visit us online at PenguinRandomHouse.com.

Library of Congress Cataloging-in-Publication Data is available.

ISBN 9780593530252

1 3 5 7 9 10 8 6 4 2

Manufactured in the United States of America

BVG

Design by Maya Tatsukawa
Text set in FS Ostro

The authorized representative in the EU for product safety and compliance is
Penguin Random House Ireland, Morrison Chambers, 32 Nassau Street,
Dublin D02 YH68, Ireland, https://eu-contact.penguin.ie.

FOR CHRISTINE ERNST BODE

1.

IT'S ALWAYS WINDY HERE.

I live on the Oregon coast in a one-hundred-year-old wooden building that was supposed to store fishing stuff. At some point, a bathroom was put in. Then later what my mom calls "the worst kitchen in the world" was added. Mom says when she closes her eyes, she smells all the years of salty, slimy fishing nets. I don't want to break it to her, but you can smell the past in here with your eyes open too.

What we call the boathouse, even if it never held a boat, sits high up the bank five hundred yards from where the Siuslaw River hits the Pacific Ocean. But when we look out the front window, we don't see water. Our view is of the Big House, which is the fancy place that the McKern family owns. This is their second home and they visit only a few times a year. In August, they always show up for ten days. That's when Oregon weather can fool a person. It's warm, but never hot. The rain and cold air go on a short summer vacation and the fog that normally pushes down on my town disappears. People drive up from California and some of them make a big mistake and buy property here. It's called "buyer's remorse" when you realize you messed up like that.

Remorse is one of the words people don't really say very much. *Re* means "again" in Latin. And *morse* comes from the Latin "to bite." So, *remorse* means to bite again, which could be the pain from something you'd like to change.

I bet the McKerns have remorse, only I'm just guessing.

Mom says we should be grateful that there are people who make popular video games in California and get fooled into thinking a big house on the Oregon coast in the small town of Florence is something they want to own, because it means that we can live at their place.

The McKerns call Mom their property manager. She doesn't get a salary, but we don't have to pay rent or any of the utility bills, and when things here break, we can use their credit card to fix them. That's good because there's a lot falling apart. One whole category of problems are the doors. The knobs, which are made of old purple glass, look great but they're always coming off. Besides that, you can only open the oven door partway because it hits the wall. And the refrigerator door is hinged in the wrong direction, so you need to squeeze into the corner to get something out. Also, the roof leaks, which is why we keep buckets on the kitchen counter. I'm used to the sound of the drips. Mom says the slope is wrong and there isn't good drainage. She must be right, because last April they took off the old roof and started over. But it didn't fix the problem.

If you have bad drainage, you will always have bad drainage.

We're supposed to be keeping an eye on the property. I do that by staring through the cloudy front window and wondering why we can't go into the Big House to watch something on one of the large TVs, or play a game of pool in what's called the "rec room." But only Mom is allowed inside. She has a routine where she walks around and checks the windows and doors. Once a day she flushes the toilets. She always turns on a few lights. She picks different ones each day to let people know things aren't just on timers. Every week she runs the water for two straight minutes in the four showers and the two bathtubs.

Plumbing, I guess like most things, doesn't do so great left alone.

The McKerns have internet, which we share, only it can be spotty for us in the boathouse. I think we should ask about getting a signal booster, but Mom says we've got a good thing going and not to complain. If I want to watch a show on Mom's computer without a lot of stopping and starting, I go sit on the Big House back deck, which looks out onto the water. It doesn't matter what time of year, I always wear my heavy coat and a knit hat and I bring a blanket. But even if it's raining (which it is most days), the overhang of the roof keeps me dry.

It's loud under the alcove. The wind comes across the sand dunes on the other side of the water and blows hard. It's like a whistle. And there's also the roaring sound of the river and the crashing of the ocean waves. The noise of rain hitting the deck of the Big House blends into the drops pinging on the Siuslaw. A drizzle on water can be louder than heavy rainfall, which doesn't seem right but has something to do with bubbles that break on the river's surface from the smaller drops. I'm not any kind of scientist, but I pay attention to things.

We didn't always live here.

Two years and four months ago we were renting a house on Buckskin Bob Road, which sounds like a joke but was the name of my old street. It was in Dunes City, just south of Florence. We were only two blocks from Siltcoos Lake. Our house was light yellow with blue trim, and our roof didn't leak. The rental had three bedrooms and there was a fenced-in backyard, which was to keep out the deer. There was old wall-to-wall carpeting that felt soft on my bare feet. We had a washer and dryer in the garage and an island in the kitchen. Mom says she never thought a kitchen island was important until we didn't have one. Two years and four and a half months ago my little brother, Geno, and I also had a dad. But on April 4, very early in the morning, there was The Accident, which is what we call what happened. If Dad hadn't been on his boat in the dark pulling up crab pots, he wouldn't have hit the sand bar, which cracked the hull of the boat, and the sneaker wave wouldn't have knocked him into the freezing water.

And everything in the world would be different.

My dad was a commercial crab fisherman, which is why his hands had a lot of calluses. He grew up in this part of Oregon and he was carrying on his family's tradition, even though his parents had moved away. Dad's mother and father got divorced when he was little and his mom moved to Alaska after he finished high school. He was an only child. Pop-Pop, my grandfather, turned the crabbing business over to Dad once he thought he was ready. After that, Pop-Pop got rid of his stuff, gave Dad his truck, and rode off on a motorcycle that had a lot of chrome. I was little and didn't understand. I guess I still don't. I remember Pop-Pop, but I guess what I'm remembering are pictures I've seen, not the real person. Mom wasn't able to find Pop-Pop to tell him about The Accident. Sometimes I think that's better because for Pop-Pop, Dad is still alive (even though I wonder how close they really were—it's not like he's been checking in on any of us).

    Mom didn't grow up here. Her family is from Coos Bay, which is also on the coast but an hour's drive south. They weren't water people. They worked driving logging trucks. But none of them are in Coos Bay anymore. One of Mom's brothers, Caleb, moved up to Spokane, Washington, and Uncle Mike and his wife split up and he lives in Texas now. After her brothers left, Mom's parents bought a used RV and they started traveling around, mostly in Arizona. Mom says that when you get older you can only take so much sadness and you don't think your heart will hold out if you hear any more bad news. I don't know if that's what happened, but they didn't come back after The Accident. They told Mom to move us to Arizona. Grandma Carol said they weren't going to spend another minute being "rainy-day people." It's too bad because my little brother and I could use a grandma and grandpa or some aunts, uncles, and cousins.

After The Accident we put Dad's ashes in the Siuslaw River under the bridge. Geno thinks this means most of him settled down into the sandy bottom, but I watched the gray powder float away on top of the water. I think it washed straight out into the ocean, because he would have wanted that.

    My father used to say I was a Daughter of the Sea. He

meant it in a good way because he loved the ocean and he was hoping he'd passed that feeling down to me.

Only I don't love the sea.

I used to be okay with it, but since The Accident I'm afraid of the waves.

My little brother, Geno, likes to throw sticks into the river and watch them get swept away. I wonder if he's thinking about Dad, but I never ask. Geno is more than four years younger than me and he doesn't have red hair like I do. Or gray eyes. When someone is talking about him, they usually say "Geno is the sweetest boy." I would find this super annoying, except it's true. He is sweet and I guess either you're born that way or you're not. Geno's real name is Genesis, which is a brand of car and an old rock band and a famous religious writing. It's also a healthcare system, a chain of gyms, and a company that makes loudspeakers.

We call him Geno because it's less confusing, but we're not Italian.

I'm lucky that my name doesn't have that kind of history.

I've never heard of anyone with the name Cordy, so I have to repeat it a bunch of times when I first meet someone. My actual name is Cordelia, but no one on the planet has ever called me that. I like my name, even though every now and then someone calls me Corky.

That is *not* okay.

I wish there was the letter z in my name. That letter is

worth ten points in Scrabble. I always hope I get the *z* tile when I play that game. If you have a *z* in your name, it might mean you're lucky.

Until The Accident, I never thought much about good luck or bad luck. Now it's always on my mind. What happened to my dad was very, very, very bad luck.

I'm waiting for a run of very, very, very *good* luck.

I try to force myself to believe that could happen.

We've been on a roll of bad luck for a while now.

Before The Accident, Mom had been taking classes at Lane Community College. She'd been studying to be a nurse. Once we lost Dad, we stayed too long at the yellow rental house and she had to quit school. There wasn't a savings account, and we didn't have life insurance. That was bad planning. I don't remember ever hearing about savings or insurance until it seemed like that's all anyone who came over to sit with Mom on the tan couch wanted to talk about.

Then we got a break because Fern Robateau needed a knee replacement and Mom was hired to do her job as a waitress at Curly's Seafood. The people there liked Mom so much that even when Fern could bend her knee again, they kept Mom on staff. A lot of people want to work at Curly's because it's known for serving the best food for miles. It's just under the Siuslaw River Bridge right on the water in what's known as Florence's Old Town. The restaurant is famous for clam chowder, which isn't my favorite because I don't like thick soup. It's like eating gravy. And also, it can be gritty. That's from the sand in the clams, not an ingredient in the recipe. Mom says people love it, only I wonder if they just pretend to.

Once something is accepted as being special, it's hard to convince people they might be wrong.

Mom says the secret ingredient in the recipe is whipping cream, but not to tell. That's why it's thick, but also sugary. At Curly's, the cooks put that in the Tenderloin Steak Diane too. But hardly anybody orders meat there.

Florence, Oregon, has a lot of retired people and tourists just passing through. When I ask why, Mom says that the logging business went away and the fishing isn't what it used to be. Plus, people don't like small towns very much anymore. She gets a look on her face and I know she's talking about herself. Since The Accident, she's been planning on finding a way out of here. This place is nearly all Geno and I have ever known, so it doesn't feel very good to hear that she's got an escape plan. But Mom is happier right now because we're heading into summer. That means there will be a line to eat at Curly's and she can make three times as much money as she does in the winter. She's all about her bank account. She's saving so we can "make a life change."

Just thinking about that gives me a stomachache.

Mom had just started working at Curly's when her

friend Taffy came in and told her that a family from California had bought the fancy property on Shoreline Drive right where the river meets the ocean, and they were looking for someone to live in their boathouse and take care of things. Taffy told the people she would send Casey Jenkins right over and that Casey would be a perfect fit.

Taffy is good at persuading people. She does phone sales.

When I first heard about all this, I imagined we'd be moving into a place with fancy models of boats, like the kind Stuart Little sailed in Central Park. The boathouse would be fixed up with pretty furniture and amazing views, and all that open river water would feel so close you'd believe you could reach out and touch it. But at the same time, you'd be far enough away to feel safe from the ocean's waves.

I got that wrong.

I'm guessing when the McKerns heard someone named Casey Jenkins was interested in living for free in their boathouse and looking after things, they imagined Casey Jenkins would be a strong guy who drove a pickup truck filled with power tools and he'd love to fix stuff.

They got that wrong.

Instead, they got us.

2.

I GO TO SIUSLAW MIDDLE SCHOOL.

It's part of the Siuslaw School District in the coastal town of Florence, Oregon: Population 9,577. The Siuslaw were one of the tribes of the indigenous Siletz people who were the first to settle this area. All the schools here have a Viking as their mascot.

There were no Vikings in the state of Oregon.

But "cultural contradictions are part of life."

I didn't come up with that. Dad did when I asked him about the Viking thing. One of the most famous Vikings was named Ivar the Boneless. He was a choice in last year's "Famous People to Learn About" project. After I heard the name, I wasn't interested in researching the guy. I was hoping for Jane Addams, who was a "Pioneer for Social Change" and won the Nobel Peace Prize. But Riley Moshofsky was given Jane Addams. She was happy because her great-grandma was named Jane. I got Albert Einstein. I didn't pick him; he was assigned to me. I think I did a good job of telling the class about one of the most influential scientists to ever live. The quote from Mr. Einstein that I like the best is: "I have no special talent. I am only passionately curious."

I'm not sure I'm passionately curious, but I do have a lot of questions about things.

My best friend is named Button Hennigan. The name on her birth certificate is Madison Hennigan, but when she was just a baby, her dad said she was "cute as a button." And the name stuck. No one looks at a button now and thinks it's "cute," but that word in the olden days used to mean "smart." And being able to close something with a button was considered clever. At least that's what I read. Somewhere along the line, *cute* changed to mean "pretty" or "sweet." Button is always worried someone will shorten her name, which happened when a boy named Carl Eddy liked her. Luckily, he moved away after third grade. Button has been a big help since The Accident. She understands when I'm feeling empty or sad inside. There are a lot of days when it's like I'm carrying an invisible backpack filled with sand.

There is only one problem with having Button as a

best friend and that's the fact that she's in a swim club. Almost every weekend she goes somewhere with her team. She does the crawl and the backstroke. Button has two things that make her a faster swimmer than other kids her age: her long arms and big feet. She wears size ten shoes and says she would be mad about having what she calls clown feet, only she thinks it's the secret to her swimming success.

Button wants to one day go to the Olympics. I bet she makes it. I tell her all the time that it's in her future. Before Button started swimming every day, we'd always do something after school, but now I go home by myself. I'm okay with that. I use that time to think about Dad.

Mom says we will always be recovering from The Accident because there's no getting over what we lost.

It's a two-mile walk from school to the boathouse. Sometimes I head over to the elementary school, which is right next to the middle school. Geno waits for me out front by the flagpole. But most days he wants to go home with his friend Jose, and I walk back to the boathouse alone.

Today Geno has one of his playdates with Jose, so he isn't with me. I head up to Thirty-fifth Street and make a left when I hear a bunch of squeaks behind me and realize I'm being followed. I turn to see a little dog on the sidewalk. He isn't too close, and at first, I think he's gotten out of a yard. I keep walking, but by the time I make it to

Shoreline Drive, the little dog is still trailing me. I stop and shout really loud, "Go home!"

My voice comes out angry even though I'm not mad, I'm just trying to make a strong point.

I watch the dog's small ears, which are perfect triangles, go flat against his head. He looks scared. I feel bad for yelling at him, but Shoreline is a busy street and I don't want to be responsible if he runs out in front of a car.

I look more closely and I can see the dog is really thin. I wonder when he last ate something. Then I remember I have half of my peanut butter sandwich left over from lunch. I pinch off a piece, crouch down low, and hold out the bread. The little dog runs right up and lunges at the food. He's frantic so he must be really hungry. I look into his eyes and I see sadness, which I know about.

I ask him, "Are you lost?"

Obviously, he doesn't answer.

But he does make a small squeak.

The little dog is soaking wet. He doesn't have a collar and his legs and belly are really dirty. His fur is matted, like he's been lying down in the mud for a long time. He isn't a puppy. He has gray hairs around his eyes and all over his muzzle. I squat lower and feed him the rest of the sandwich, piece by piece. When he's done, he eats the two carrot sticks I have in the bottom of my lunch sack. It seems like they're hard for him to chew, but he still gobbles them up. That's how hungry he is.

After he's done eating, he leans against my leg and his head rests on my left knee. Through my jeans I can feel him trembling. That does it. I pick up the little dog and carry him under my arm like a football. He keeps lifting his head to stare at me; his black eyes look so grateful. He has a wet nose and bad breath, but I still think he's perfect.

The first thing I do when I get to the boathouse is put him in the kitchen sink and give him a bath. I use real shampoo. I want the little guy to look as good as possible when he meets Mom. I wouldn't say he likes it, but he never once snarls at me, even when I take a comb and pull on the tangled parts of his fur. After two shampoos, I get some of Mom's hair conditioner. It makes him, like the bottle says, "soft and silky."

Once he's clean, I lift him out of the sink and he does a bunch of tip-to-tail shakes, sending water drops flying everywhere. Then he settles down to lick his legs and paws. I dry off his body as best I can and then find Mom's blow-dryer. He doesn't like the noise and his tail goes between his legs, so I decide he's dry enough.

The little dog doesn't have a collar, but a few days ago the strap broke on my backpack. It wasn't in great shape and Mom said it wasn't worth fixing, but I remember it didn't get thrown away. I take scissors and cut through the nylon, which has a buckle, and I make it into a little dog collar. It's clean and dry and looks pretty good. Then I take a pillow from the couch, cover it with a towel, and put it in our laundry basket. I lift the little guy down onto the pillow. He could get out if he tried, but he just watches me and I know he's trying to do the right thing. I take one of the heaters from the room I share with Geno, and I aim it at the basket. Then I sit down on the floor beside him, and I start humming. I used to sing all the time, but I don't feel like doing that very much anymore. Maybe because my dad had a great voice and we would sing together a lot. At night I hum songs to Geno to help him fall asleep. When he was really little, my brother was afraid of moths. He said they were evil, dusty night butterflies. Now neither of us likes the dark, because that's what the sky was like when we woke up and heard about The Accident.

By the time I hear our truck pull into the driveway, the little lost dog is warm and dry and sound asleep. Only as soon as Mom comes through the door, he jumps up, knocks over the laundry basket, and starts barking like a maniac. He might be some kind of watch dog. It's like he's more worried about the property than any of us are.

Mom acts like she's looking at a moose. "Cordy, what's that dog doing in here?"

"He's lost. He started following me home from school. I couldn't let him get run over by a car. I was trying to do the right thing."

Mom isn't happy. She bends down and looks closely. "He's no puppy, that's for sure." Her eyes are soft, but she doesn't pet him. I lift him up. He's smart because he seems to understand that the boss is in the room. He keeps his eyes on Mom. He opens his mouth and he might be trying to smile. I say, "He doesn't shed."

"All dogs shed."

I can't tell her I gave him a bath in the kitchen sink and that's how I know that almost none of his fur came out. I'm holding him and he's wagging his tail and trying to be super friendly.

Mom sighs. "We've got to find his owner. Someone's probably really worried. His collar looks clean, but there aren't any tags?"

"Nope. No tags. Nothing. He might be abandoned."

"He smells good. Someone's been taking care of him."

He smells like her shampoo and conditioner, but she doesn't recognize it. And she also doesn't realize his collar is my backpack strap.

Our town is small, but people move here all the time and just as many leave and they don't always take their pets when they go. I guess they figure someone will step in. A lot of people can barely take care of themselves, and maybe a pet gets to be more than they can handle.

I don't want to judge anyone, but when I was in third grade, I saw a woman in a red car pull into the parking lot in the back of Fred Meyer, which is the biggest store in town. I was waiting in the truck for Dad, who ran in to get some cough syrup for Geno. The red car was packed with boxes and there were two bikes on the back and stuff tied down under a blue tarp on the roof. The woman opened the passenger door and dropped a handful of stuff. I watched as two dogs jumped out and started eating the treats. Then the woman slammed the door shut and she drove away, moving faster than you're supposed to in a parking lot.

I felt so bad for the dogs, but I also felt bad for the lady. No one would want to be that kind of person.

I wanted to get out and go after the dogs, but we had a strict rule not to leave the car. I tried to see where they went when they finished eating the treats, but the parking lot was crowded and I lost sight of them.

As soon as Dad came back, I told him what happened. He started shaking his head and then he said "Some people . . ." but he never finished the sentence. We drove all around the parking lot and then the streets near the store searching, but we didn't find them. Since then, whenever we shop at Fred Meyer, I look for those dogs. But I've never seen them.

I look for my dad every day in that same way, thinking maybe he's just around the corner.

I hope those dogs found a new home.

It isn't long after Mom is back that Geno gets dropped off from his playdate. He starts crying right after he comes in because he's so happy that we finally got a dog. Then he cries harder when Mom says we aren't keeping him because he's obviously lost and belongs to someone. She takes a picture on her phone and makes a flyer on her computer to locate his owners. We don't have a printer to make copies and Mom says she doesn't want to use up the ink in the one the McKerns have, so we'll go to print shop.

I whisper to Geno not to worry as we all climb into Dad's old truck. The dog sits on my lap in the laundry basket on the drive to Printland. Geno stays in the truck with his arm around the basket while Mom and I go inside. He says he doesn't want the little dog to be left alone in the dark.

Ernie Burke is working behind the counter. He knew Dad and he says he's not going to charge us to make flyers because we're doing a good thing by trying to find the lost dog's owner. He also gives us plastic sleeves for free and he lets us borrow his staple gun.

It's a windy night, but we put LOST DOG signs on telephone poles on the streets all around where the dog found me. The LOST part is the biggest thing you can see on the flyer and the picture Mom took is right above it. Geno says, "It looks like his name is Lost."

We all laugh because I tell them that the first thing I said to the little guy was, "Are you lost?"

After that, we just start calling him Lost.

This amazing dog was lost and then he got found, which might have been a better thing to name the little guy.

I say to Mom, "What if Lost is good luck for us?"

Mom just shakes her head. "I don't believe in good luck."

I want to ask if she believes in bad luck, but I don't.

I take Lost and I hold him against my chest. I don't want to crush him but I want him close. I've wanted a dog for as long as I can remember, and the answer was always no. Dad used to explain that when I was old enough to take care of an animal, things would be different. Just before The Accident, Dad said the time was right, but then everything changed and we moved out of the house on Buckskin Bob and Mom had her hands full. Getting a dog was "not in the cards."

I don't play cards.

But Mom says that Lost is a wild card and that someone might call and claim him. We wait in the truck while Mom goes into the store to buy a small bag of dog food and a leash. I feel like she should have bought a bigger bag, but it's a start.

Dad said that once you start feeding an animal, you've taken responsibility.

We are going to go home, but we're all so hungry that Mom stops at the A & W and we decide to eat in the car. Mom doesn't like us to eat fast food, so it feels special. We used to come here with Dad and we haven't been back since The Accident. I don't want to wreck anything by pointing this out. Geno and I split a root beer float and Mom even takes a sip, which she never does. She says she's the only person on the planet who doesn't have a sweet tooth. Then Geno says, "It feels like we're celebrating something."

I know what he means. I say, "We are celebrating finding Lost."

Mom is chewing her french fries, but she stops and says, "Kids, we'll probably hear from his owners tomorrow."

Lost looks up with his big dark eyes. He's staring right at Mom.

"He's trying to tell you something," says Geno.

"He's saying he wants a french fry," I explain, which makes Mom laugh.

"But no ketchup."

Geno doesn't like ketchup.

If Lost could talk, I bet he'd have a lot to say about his bath and his fake collar. I think he'd explain he's an older dog and he didn't escape from a yard. He got kicked out of somewhere. Or just left behind.

Then he lets out a single bark and that makes us laugh. For some reason, we can't stop. I think it's because we're all tired and we are at the A & W in the rain eating in the car and it feels like we're a normal family again.

When we get home, Geno shows he's so kind. He says, "You found Lost, so he should sleep with you tonight." I think we all want him. Even Mom. She picks up the little dog and Lost sits on her lap on the couch while we get ready for bed. He licks her face, which might be because he smells salt from her french fries, but Geno says, "He's giving you a kiss."

When it's time to go to sleep, I put Lost down at the foot of my bed and I go get a drink of water. When I come back, he's got his head on my pillow and his eyes are closed. Mom comes in and watches me lean over to kiss his nose.

"Cordy, don't get too attached. We might hear from his owners tomorrow."

I'm not that worried. But I tell her, "It's okay. I'll love him for as long as he's with us."

Mom turns out the light and whispers, "Good night, kids."

Maybe it wasn't the right thing to say, because I could hear that the sadness in her voice had returned.

3.

IT RAINED HARD ALL NIGHT.

But in the morning, the sun comes out, which is a rare thing to see when I wake up. I think it's a good sign. We decide that Lost will be okay staying in the house while we're gone. I'm going to worry about him even though he looks pretty happy when we leave. He's had his breakfast and gone outside to check the property. He ran all around the deck on the Big House. I think he was impressed. At first, we put him on the leash, but Mom decided he didn't look like he would run off. We watched as he did his business, after sniffing the pine needles and the trunks of the fir trees like a detective. It made me look at the ground in a new way. There's a lot going on right under our feet.

In the car driving to school, I see that all the flyers we put up have blown away. I don't say anything, but neither does Mom. I'm excited for my first class, which is science, because Button will be there. As soon as I see her, I start talking.

"Guess what! We got a dog yesterday!"

"Really, Cordy?" She understands how much this means to me. Her family has a dog, two cats, and a parakeet.

"This little stray followed me home. Mom's okay with keeping him until we find the owner. But I don't think that's going to happen."

Button's face changes. "Maybe you shouldn't get too attached. You know, in case–"

"That's what Mom says. But when I found him, he was all dirty and starving to death and–"

I have to stop because Mrs. Bingham walks in and she's pretty strict about no talking once class has started. I whisper, "I'll tell you more at lunch." Button gives me a thumbs-up. She doesn't just have big feet. Her hands are kind of large too. She's taller than me, and most of the boys in our grade too. She's got a big skeleton.

We are born into our bodies and we don't get to pick them.

I have big ears, but my hair hides them. I eat a lot, but I'm on the skinny side. So is Mom. Geno is more like Dad. He was what Mom called stocky. He was strong and his back was wide. Certain things are passed down to us. My red hair comes from both sides of my family, even though Mom and Dad aren't redheads.

I wonder about Lost's parents. He looks like a mutt, a mix of different kinds of dogs rather than one kind of breed. I'm thinking about all of this instead of earth and space, which is what our teacher Mrs. Bingham is talking about. I blink and imagine Lost wearing a spacesuit. I'd like to draw a picture of that, but instead I force myself to concentrate.

Button wants to see my new dog, so after school I wait for her mom, who comes four days a week to take Button to swim practice. Mrs. Hennigan agrees to drive me home so Button can meet Lost even though it means she'll be late to the pool.

At the Big House, Button jumps out of the car and runs inside with me. Lost is barking like crazy. But he must realize that Button is a good friend, because he stops when she picks him up to get a good look.

"Cordy, I love him!"

"I love him too."

"He's perfect!"

"He's *so* perfect."

Button's nose twitches. "He has kind of bad breath." She laughs. I laugh. I feel like Lost would laugh if he could. Button puts him down. "I wish I could stay, but—"

She doesn't even finish before we hear her mom's car horn.

"Swim practice."

"Thanks for coming to see him." I scoop up Lost and we walk outside together. I go to the car and Mrs. Hennigan rolls down the window. She's smiling before she even gets a good look at my new dog. "I'm happy for you, Cordy."

I can tell she means it.

The next day, Mom says we have to go to the humane society and leave one of the flyers in case someone is looking for Lost. I know it's the right thing to do, but it makes me worried. I can see that Mom is worried too. We don't tell Geno. He has started calling Lost his little brother.

When Mom walks out of the building, she's upset. "Okay, if someone comes and claims Lost, we can think about getting ourselves a rescue dog. There are a lot in there that need homes."

Before, this would have been huge news because we've broken the barrier of getting a dog.

But now I only nod.

I don't want any dog but Lost.

For the next ten days I go to sleep and I wake up with a new thing to worry about. But maybe it's not all bad because instead of thinking about Dad, I can spiral into imagining Mom's cell phone ringing and someone saying that we have their Lost dog, named Martin. Sometimes they call and ask if we have Milo. It's always a dog with an *M* name. Maybe because they say their dog is *m*issing. But the call doesn't come.

And after two weeks, I stop worrying so much.

Lost has a few funny habits and one is that he likes empty plastic bottles. We don't buy water that way, and Mom won't let us have soft drinks, but Lost somehow finds plastic containers when he's outside. He brings them back to the house and leaves them by the front door. Maybe in his former life he worked at a recycling center. It's just one more reason to love him.

Mom says the good thing about a small town is that everyone knows everyone's business. If someone was looking for Lost, we'd hear about it.

By the end of the month, we realize the little dog with the stinko breath is ours now. Mom agrees that he's part of the family and she buys the biggest bag of dog food. She's a planner, so that says it all.

Lost barks at everything he hears.

And he hears everything. This makes him a twenty-four-hour alarm system, which can be irritating. It doesn't usually bother me that much, but on Saturday morning we should be sleeping in. Lost doesn't understand the days of the week.

I want Mom to have extra rest, so I get up and let Lost out to do his business. He's learned to be quick. I don't call his name; if I snap my fingers, he will run to the boathouse. I have him trained. After he's inside, he will stay by the front door because his workday has started. He's got to be alert for possible bad guys. A squirrel qualifies.

But this morning is different.

I let Lost out, and he doesn't come back.

I wait.

Finally, I step onto the little muddy pebbles in front of the door, which are always wet. I don't see him anywhere. I pull on my rain boots and grab my green coat, put it on and pull up the hood. I'm still in my nightgown. Dad always wore a waterproof yellow rain hat when he was on the boat. Geno says it was the same kind as Paddington the Bear has.

Mom gave away almost all of Dad's clothes when we moved from Buckskin Bob, because she said they should be used, not stored in boxes getting moldy. But she kept his favorite blue sweater, his good leather belt, and his slippers. I asked if I could keep his big green hoodie and his fishing hat. Geno was too little to know what he'd want, so Mom put aside one of Dad's flannel shirts and his big brown work boots. Later Geno asked if he could put dirt in them and grow flowers. Mom said no.

I look down at my rain boots. Where is Lost? It's cold and spitting rain, which is what we call a drizzle that stops and starts from the gray sky. I snap my fingers and look around, but no dog. I go up to the Big House, which Lost likes to check out, even though it's always empty. The last time someone was there besides Mom or me was five months ago when the McKerns came up with their French bulldog named Pierre. Lost must still be able to smell the Frenchie, because he heads straight for the front door to do what looks like the kind of police search and seizure operation I've seen on TV. He charges onto the deck and then circles with his nose down. His legs get stiff like he's mad. The McKerns' dog Pierre has breathing problems and does a lot of snorting. His bark sounds like a scream. He's a good dog, but nothing like Lost, who is an amazing dog, with only one bad quality and that's his stinko breath.

Mom told me that Pierre eats rotisserie chicken that gets cut up special just for him. Brown rice and steamed broccoli are mixed in. Mom watched his dinner being made when she was in the Big House kitchen taking notes from the McKerns about stuff they want her to do while they're gone. Also, Pierre doesn't drink tap water. He gets his bowl filled from the water that comes in square bottles. Dad used to say that water was for suckers. Pierre has a fancy red collar that has shiny metal hearts pressed into the leather and he wears a sweater when he goes outside. He owns three different kinds. One is light blue and covered with little white clouds. I would like that sweater in my size. Whenever Pierre is outside doing his business, he has to always be on a leash.

I feel bad because I think Pierre would like to run free. Also, I wonder how he really feels about his sweaters.

But I understand that this property isn't fenced and maybe he'd take off.

Lost would never do that. At least, I didn't think he would until today, because I can't find him.

I don't want to wake up anyone, but I finally cup my hands together and yell "LOST!"

He doesn't come.

I start to get a bad feeling.

There are a lot of wild animals around this place. There are Roosevelt elk, which are named after President Theodore Roosevelt, and some of them weigh almost nine hundred pounds. They have antlers that could make big trouble for a little dog. The same with black-tailed deer, who look cute but wouldn't like a dog chasing after them. Plus, coyotes roam at night and sometimes in the early morning they are still looking to catch mice and rabbits, or knock over trash cans and pick through the garbage. We hear them yipping in packs when they are hunting. We have eagles and osprey, and they can go after an old dog too, especially one as small as Lost. And there are bobcats and mountain lions that live upstream where the river has woods on both sides.

Three hours north of here, a mountain lion got stranded on Haystack Rock, which is a famous place for tourists to take pictures. It looks like a big haystack coming up out of the water. The rock is what's called a sea stack, which are slabs of stone. When I heard the mountain lion was stuck out there, I tried to figure out what happened. Maybe the big cat walked across the sand at low tide at night. There are tidepools there filled with crabs and mussels and other things that are good to eat. Or maybe the mountain lion chased a deer down to the beach and it darted toward Haystack to get away.

A man who was camping took a picture of the mountain lion in the early morning and showed the park ranger. That's when all the publicity started. The state closed the area and made people stay away. Newspeople showed up from Eugene to try to get pictures. They gave the story a name, which was "The Cat on the Rock." But by the next morning, the cougar was gone. So it worked out. Now you can buy coffee cups at the tourist places around Cannon Beach with a picture of the mountain lion on the third-highest sea stack in the world.

I stop thinking about all of this and remember I'm looking for Lost.

When I get to the back deck of the Big House, which faces the river, I call out again, but this time really loud. I shout "LOST!" in a long cry that is mostly "LAAAAWWW-WWW" with a "ST!" added in at the end. It actually takes all the air I have in my lungs.

I take a breath and try to calm down.

Without my new little dog with the bad breath, I'm

going to fall apart. I try calling again, this time more shrieking than shouting.

And then I hear something.

Lost has the kind of high-pitched bark that can be annoying. Right now, it sounds like the best thing I've ever heard. I move to the edge of the deck and I realize his yapping is coming from the river. We're not supposed to go down there. The McKerns have a dock, but they don't have a boat and Mom says there's no reason to be that close to the river. I'm afraid, so she doesn't need to tell me to stay away. But now I take off in a run toward the water.

There's a gravel trail that zigzags down the steep slope. Trees are on either side, with ferns and blackberry brambles so overgrown that the actual path is hard to see. My feet, in the rain boots with no socks, slide around and I come close to face-planting. All kinds of bad things race through my mind, including what I'd do if I fell and broke my leg or something worse.

When I get to the bottom I see Lost standing out on the end of the dock. He's right at the edge. And he's barking his head off, but the sound of the moving water makes it like he's on mute.

I don't want to be this close to the river. But I'm so happy my little dog is okay. I start yelling. "LOST! What are you doing?" He keeps right on barking. I step onto the dock and discover why he's excited. At first, I think there are a bunch of harbor seals in the water. They make their way up the river all the time and some live under the bridge by Old Town. People feed them, which they shouldn't.

But as I move down the dock, I realize I'm not looking at seals.

There's a pod of dolphins out there!

They've left the ocean and come up the river. I watch as they leap in arcs out of the gray water. I count at least ten different ones, but I bet there are more. I know these are bottlenose dolphins. Back when we went out on Dad's boat one summer, we'd seen a pod like this off the coast. Dad said it was lucky.

I didn't know that dolphins could come up the river.

It feels like magic.

Lost probably has never seen dolphins. And they are so close. Maybe he thinks they are swimming dogs. He barks every time one of them breaks the surface of the water, and he really loses his mind when they leap high into the air, showing off their gray faces and white bellies. The dolphins have such smooth skin and I can see their front flippers, which look like oven mitts. The line of their mouths is long, making it seem like they are smiling. They swim so close that I can see the blowholes on the tops of their heads. That's how they breathe.

I forget that I'm only wearing my nightgown.

I forget that it's windy and my red hair is swirling into tangles that will hurt to brush out.

I forget that my dad is gone after his boat hit a sand bar very close to where I'm standing.

I forget that I'm afraid of the dock and the river and the ocean.

All I know is that maybe *I am* a Daughter of the Sea, because suddenly there is something that makes me stop breathing: One of the dolphins, a small one, is pink.

This little pink dolphin leaps up out of the water and then disappears back into the river. I figure I must have just seen a shadow or the morning light is playing a trick on me. I wait for the dolphin's head to come up again and when it does, I know I'm not imagining it. Because she's pink, it's easier to see her dark eyes. They stand out against her light body.

I shriek, but in a good way. It's like I'm on the Scrambler at the county fair. I don't think I've made this kind of noise since then.

The dolphins must be eating a school of fish. I watch until there's a change. Did the fish below scatter? Suddenly the dolphins are moving. I realize they've headed down the river back out to the ocean. I stand blinking on the dock. I've never seen dolphins in the Siuslaw. And I've never heard of a pink dolphin.

There are times when the Siuslaw looks so big and strong flowing out into the sea. But the river changes direction with high tide and that's why it's an estuary, which is when fresh water mixes with salt. The moon controls what happens. When I was little, Dad explained that a tide just means changing water level. He said it's always going forward or going back. It has to do with gravity, which is another thing that is super interesting but almost hurts your head if you think about it for too long.

Dad knew all about the tides.

I wish I could remember everything he told me. But one thing that sticks out is that in a super high tide, the level of the Siuslaw is affected for twenty-six miles upstream. He wasn't making that up. He understood so many things.

I want to tell Dad about the dolphins.

I want to tell him that I have a dog now and his name is Lost and he brought me down here to the dock.

I want to tell him I stood out here and I saw what's called an anomaly of nature, which was a pink dolphin.

I want to tell him I wasn't afraid.

4.

LOST STOPS BARKING BECAUSE THE DOLPHINS ARE GONE.

He looks worn out.

We both are.

I start back up the steep trail with Lost at my heels. We are soaking wet. The wind blows hard and my little dog is shivering. My knees, just below my nightgown, look blue. It's the beginning of June and I know that in a lot of places it probably feels like summer. The days get longer here, but the change in the seasons doesn't make that much difference until at least July. The rain and the wind and the cold are what keep everything green. People say the weather is why there aren't big hotels and restaurants and tons of tourists here.

I wish that Lost could talk to me. He's the one who came down to the dock and saw the dolphins. I stop to take his little head in my hands and I say, "There were dolphins in the river. One of them was pink. You were my witness." I feel like he understands every word, only maybe that's not true, because he runs and gets a stick and brings it to me. I bet he'd rather have an empty plastic bottle. Lost looks happy as he marches ahead of me, holding his prize. We make it back up to the boathouse and I try to be extra quiet. I go to the bathroom to towel off and I try to dry Lost. He's still got the stick and he won't let go, which makes it harder. I realize I'm shaking from the cold. My teeth start to chatter. I put on stretch pants and then jeans over them. I get into a T-shirt and layer it with a heavy sweater, then I sit down on the old wooden floor right next to one of our portable heaters. The planks are scratched and beaten down, but I think in a good way.

It smells like fish in here.

I'm still cold, but excited because I have a new thing to investigate: I want to know more about dolphins.

I take Mom's computer and stand close to the front window with the wavy glass. I type in *pink dolphin*. I find out that a pink dolphin is an albino. I read that all mammals have a specific gene that scientists have named TYR. An animal can have something off in their TYR gene, and so they don't make melanin, which is what gives cells color that shows up in skin and hair and eyes. An albino is born white, but the sun causes changes. In parts of the Amazon where it's fresh water, there are many pink river dolphins. They are called botos. They're in Peru, Venezuela, Brazil, Bolivia, Colombia, and Ecuador, but they are different from what I saw today.

Once Mom is awake and she's had her coffee, I ask if I can go to the library. It's on Ninth Street and I've been checking out books there since I was in kindergarten. Mom looks happy about this. "Sounds good, Boo. I'll drop you guys off on the way to work."

I like it when she calls me Boo. She sometimes calls Geno Bud.

Dad called us those names.

If we're Boo and Bud, she's in a good mood.

Mom's got the lunch *and* the dinner shift today. Saturdays are usually the restaurant's busiest time of the week because people drive to the coast from Eugene and Corvallis. Both of those cities are more than an hour away. They are what Mom calls "college towns." We've been to Eugene a ton of times, but I don't think it's that exciting. Most visitors from these places come here for one or two nights to have clam chowder and walk on the beach. Some only stay for the day. But they can leave good tips at the restaurant.

Mom talks a lot lately about us moving to Eugene or

Corvallis. She starts up on that again as she folds laundry. "When we move, I won't work on weekends."

Geno looks up from his cereal. He doesn't like hearing about moving. He would miss his best friend, Jose. But he doesn't say anything. Mom keeps talking. "There's so much more opportunity in a bigger place."

I want to say, "Opportunity to do what?"

There's no ocean.

No sand dunes.

No river. Okay, there might be a river, because I remember a bridge in Eugene.

There would be no friend like Button.

There would be no dolphins.

But I don't say that.

Dad is in the water and we shouldn't leave him.

Mom keeps folding. She's mostly talking to herself, so she doesn't expect an answer. "If we didn't have a free place to live here, we'd go right away. I'm saving up. That's why we don't throw money around. Once I can get enough ahead, I'm going to make it happen. I'll finish my nursing degree and apply for a job at a real hospital and I won't come home smelling like fried food."

Geno half smiles. "I like the smell of fried food."

Mom puts her hand on his head and says, "Sweet Geno." She goes to the sink in the worst kitchen in the world and rinses out her coffee cup. "You can take sandwiches to the library. Maybe it will be nice and you can sit outside. I'm making you guys spaghetti for dinner. Cordy, all you need to do is heat it up. I'll also steam some spinach."

I nod. Me and Geno will have the spaghetti, but give Lost the spinach. He eats anything, especially if it has butter on top. Lost might have 'food insecurity," which is real if you've found yourself hungry a lot in the past. He does have his dog food, which he eats in the morning and at night, but in between he's always up for any "people food" he can manage to get. He even eats broccoli stems and apple cores, which is weird for a dog. If he knew about the Frenchie named Pierre in the Big House with his rotisserie chicken meals, he'd probably go nuts.

Mom's a mind reader. "And don't give your spinach to the dog. He might get diarrhea."

Geno and I look at each other and laugh. *Diarrhea* is such a funny word. Because we are laughing, Lost rushes over and leans his head against Geno's leg. He's making his move to get the leftover milk in Geno's cereal bowl.

My little brother didn't cause a fuss about the library because he's a sweet kid. As Mom says, "He goes along to get along." I'm pretty sure Geno would rather go to Jose's, but he's off on a camping trip this weekend, so he's stuck with me.

Mom leaves to take a shower. Once she's out of the room, I say to Geno, "I know you don't really want to go to the library." Geno shrugs. He puts his cereal bowl on the floor and lets Lost lap up the leftover milk. Dairy products aren't good for dogs, but I don't think a little bit is that bad, so I don't say anything.

"I promise I'll try to get Mom to take us to Dairy Queen tomorrow."

Geno looks up in a hopeful way. "Why can't we go today?"

"It's the wrong direction from the library. It will make the walk home longer."

"Not that much longer. And I love Dairy Queen. Because of the Blizzards."

"I know you do."

"I dream about them."

"Which means you have sweet dreams."

"Most of the time. But I also dream about zombies."

"Zombies aren't real."

"They are in my dreams."

He has a point. Then he adds, "I love the strawberry cheesecake Blizzard." He looks concerned. "I hope they always have that flavor."

"Don't worry. They will," I say, and then feel guilty. How do I know what changes might happen to a Dairy Queen menu item? But Geno smiles really wide. Even his eyes are smiling.

"Thanks, Cordy."

I nod.

I figured out one thing in the last two years: The secret to being a good big sister is to make the world less scary.

Mom gets to wear whatever she wants to work, but she has to always have on an orange apron when she's waiting tables, and a black baseball cap that says *Keep Clam and Carry On*. It's supposed to be a joke. Geno always says "I don't understand why that's funny." Mom agrees. Plus, she says she doesn't look good in baseball caps, but she's wrong. She looks good in anything. While she's getting ready to go, I head to the top shelf in the kitchen to get my money, which I'm saving for a good birthday present for Button. I'm thinking of ordering a Northern Galaxy light projector, which would shine stars up onto the ceiling. I keep my savings in a box of oatmeal packets. It feels like a safe place because no robber would want instant oatmeal. *We* don't even want it.

I have twenty-nine dollars and twenty-five cents from doing errands and pulling weeds over at Old Mrs. Crowley's house. That's what everyone calls her: Old Mrs. Crowley. I wonder at what point the *Old* part got added to her name. She lives right next door to Button, which is how I know her. Button used to do the odd jobs, but now that she's training every day to go to the Olympics, I got called in as the backup.

Old Mrs. Crowley has macular degeneration, so she can't see well enough to do her own yardwork. But she still wants the dandelions and the crab grass ripped out of her rose garden. Whenever I'm over there, she takes a folding chair off her small porch and she sits on her little walkway while I do the work. She has a pink umbrella, which she holds in the rain. She looks like one of the people I've seen on TV at golf tournaments. Only she's not watching a sport. She's staring out in my direction while I'm bent over her rosebushes. I'm not really sure how much she sees, but she tells me I'm doing a good job.

When we are in our truck on the way to the library, we pass Button's house. The carport is empty because they are gone for the weekend so Button can swim against tougher competition, whatever that means. Next up is Old Mrs. Crowley's little house. Through the window I can see the TV is on. She says she can't make out the picture because of her eye problems, but the voices keep her company. Old Mrs. Crowley gets audiobooks from the Braille Institute sent to her in the mail and she told me that without them she'd lose her mind. She likes to listen to biographies of interesting people. Her favorite person in the whole world is a guy named Clive Davis. He was a record producer who was orphaned as a teenager, but still went to a fancy college and then to law school. Old Mrs. Crowley never worked in the music business. She had a job at an elevator repair company in Sacramento, California, before she retired and moved to Florence. "All elevators break, you can count on that!" is all she's ever said about what she did. She claims the Clive Davis autobiography is "essential reading for all record producers." I don't want to be negative, but I don't think she's ever going to be a record producer.

After The Accident, Old Mrs. Crowley gave me my own copy of the Clive Davis book. She said she thought it might take my mind off stuff. It was a nice thing to do. I keep it on my shelf in the room I share with Geno. I started but never finished it because unlike Old Mrs. Crowley, I couldn't form a bond with Clive Davis.

Mom pulls to the curb in front of the library and Geno and I get out. My little brother watches her car go down Ninth Street to the stoplight. I don't know if she looks up into the rearview mirror to see he hasn't moved, but knowing Mom, she probably does.

I wish we could have brought Lost with us, but he's not a service animal, so he's not allowed inside. I want to tell Geno to hurry up, but I don't. Once he's finally ready, we walk together to the front doors. The big sign over the entrance says *Siuslaw Public Library*. I've never heard anyone call it that. It's just the library. They don't have a mascot, which is a relief. The only Vikings here are in books.

Saturdays are the library's biggest day and all kinds of people are inside. Geno heads to where the kids' graphic novels are kept. He likes to read about robots, superheroes, and spies. He forgets he's in the library and calls out to me, "I'll be waiting for you." Geno doesn't ever tell me to hurry. He's setting unreasonable expectations for me about the rest of the world. I doubt I'll ever find anyone who's as easygoing as he is. He was that way before The Accident and he didn't change. I did. I think I appreciate him even more now.

I head over to the reference desk. Mrs. Hunt is there. She is perfect as a research librarian because she helps people *hunt* stuff down. She speaks in a voice that's half whisper/half regular.

"Hello, Cordy."

My parents have always said that it's important for kids to have good manners. I didn't really think about it until after The Accident, but now I try to be polite because that's what Dad would have wanted. Everyone says I don't talk loud enough since we lost Dad. What's great is that in here my low voice is appropriate. "Good morning, Mrs. Hunt. How're you doing today?"

"I'm well. What can I help you with, sweetheart?"

I like that she calls me sweetheart.

I have a brown paper bag with me. Our sandwiches are inside and I'll use it to carry home the books we check out. I can see Mrs. Hunt staring at it.

"The strap on my backpack broke."

"Because you carry around so many books, Cordy."

"Yeah. Or maybe it just wore out. Mom said it wasn't very well made. I brought lunch with me."

I don't tell her we got the backpack from the second-hand store and it was already pulling apart at the seams when we bought it.

"What kind of books are you curious about today?"

"I'm doing research on dolphins. And also, on mammals that are albinos. A book on albino dolphins would be amazing."

Mrs. Hunt's face says to me that she's intrigued. But I decide not to tell her about the dolphins in the river.

"How interesting. Is this for a school report?"

"No. Only for me. These are just two random things I've been thinking about."

I probably sound like I'm lying, but Mrs. Hunt is buying what I'm selling. She smiles. "That's wonderful. I've got some ideas."

It doesn't take very long for Mrs. Hunt to find a book called *Albino Animals*. There's a picture of a white mouse with red eyes on the cover. It's for little kids, but I take it because Mrs. Hunt says there aren't a lot of materials "in this specific area." It will be a quick read. While she keeps searching, I turn the pages. It's kind of upsetting to know there are albino koala bears in the world, especially with all the sun in Australia, but once you learn something, you can't really unlearn it. Also, a koala bear isn't a bear. They are marsupials. There's so much misinformation out there. For an albino animal to be born, both parents have to carry a very rare recessive gene mutation. Mom and Dad had to each have had a recessive gene for hair color, which explains my red hair. There are no books only about albino dolphins, so Mrs. Hunt has found stuff for me about regular dolphins. These books cover the basics, like the fact that they are mammals that have to breath air every seven minutes. This means that while they live in water, they are more like us than they are like fish. Besides the breathing, another example is we both don't have scales. Because they need oxygen, but live in the ocean, dolphins don't sleep the way we do. A part of a dolphin's brain has to always be awake so that they can come up for air. Apparently, one section of the brain sleeps while the other part remembers about needing to stick their head out of the water.

In the morning, Mom sometimes forgets to take the little saucepan off the stove. It has the milk for her coffee, which burns and smells like the smoke from a campfire. I know she has a lot to worry about, but it's a good thing she doesn't have to remember to breathe. Only I'd never say that to her. She'd feel bad.

Dolphins "vocalize" by whistling, squealing, grunting, and gargling. They make these sounds through their noses. I shut my eyes and push out air as hard as I can through my nostrils. The only thing that happens is a small squeak, which frees up some snot. Luckily, I have a tissue in my coat pocket.

Humans are the smartest animals on the planet, and dolphins come in second. They are even smarter than chimpanzees. They can solve puzzles and learn games. They can be trained to do complicated things and can even remember something important for twenty years. They live in groups and they share.

I wish our school mascot was a dolphin.

I don't want to be a Viking. They are known for fighting battles.

I want to be a dolphin. They are known for protecting each other.

5.

I'M SPENDING TOO MUCH TIME WITH THE BOOKS MRS. Hunt gave me.

I look up at the clock and realize it's been almost an hour since I sat down. I can disappear into things. I should have thought about Geno. I bring the books back to the front desk. I leave the three I want to take home off to the side, and I go to get my brother.

He's not in the kids' section.

I'm surprised, but this place isn't that big, so he must be close. Dad taught us to find things in an organized way. His job was to put crab pots into the ocean, and you need a plan for that. There are buoys that mark the traps, but still, you can't just zigzag through the water looking for your catch. Dad said that when something is missing, you think of a wheel, and you start from the outside and move around circling to the center. You can also start from the center and go out.

I can't remember which way was better.

I start from the walls and move in, but there are dividers and hallways and an area that's only for staff. I don't see Geno anywhere. It's a library, so I can't shout his name.

He has to be in here.

My brother would never leave without me. He's not like that.

I'm not panicking.

Then I remember the bathrooms. I head to the men's bathroom, but I can't go in, so I wait. I don't like to talk to strangers, only I don't have a choice. A man comes out. He has a beard that's got a lot of red in it. Because I have red hair, that makes me feel better. He's wearing suspenders. Dad had fishing pants with suspenders. I say, "Excuse me, I'm trying to find my little brother. Could you go call for Geno? That's his name."

The man pushes the door open and doesn't even go inside. He just shouts, "GENO!" It's way louder than he needed to yell. It's not a very big bathroom and I can see through the open door that my brother's not there. The man wearing the suspenders shrugs. "No Geno. Sorry, kiddo."

I manage to say "Thank you."

I start to get afraid.

Where's my brother?

I need help.

I go to Mrs. Hunt at the reference desk. I forget to use a library voice and blurt out, "I can't find Geno. My little brother came in with me—"

I must be more upset than I think, because Mrs. Hunt reaches across the counter and puts her hand on my arm. "It's okay, Cordy. I'll help you find him."

Mrs. Hunt doesn't normally do anything quickly, but she moves fast. I feel better, only not for very long because she does the exact same thing I did. She just walks around in a big circle looking for Geno. I'm thinking about whether I should call Mom and say I lost my little brother in the library. It's my job to take care of him. What will she think?

What if someone took him?

He's too old to be picked up and carried out of here.

And that would be kidnapping!

But he's so nice to everyone. He might have been tricked.

Maybe someone asked him for help bringing their books to a car. Should I check the parking lot?

A bad person could have Geno.

But two terrible things can't happen to the same family. There's the law of averages, and that's just not possible.

I start to have trouble breathing. All of a sudden, I can only take little gulps of air. Then I feel my heart in my chest. It has only pounded like this after I've been running. My eyes fill up with tears.

I'm not going to cry. I'm way too old for that.

I turn away from the front desk and head into a hallway so that I can lean against the wall. A door there opens. A plaque on the wall reads: THE BROMLEY MEETING ROOM. Two women come out. I move to the open doorway and look inside. There are a lot of people getting up from blue folding chairs. A man in rust-colored pants and a striped shirt is standing next to a smart board. I read the words SIUSLAW VISION. Underneath it says: BUILDING A BETTER COMMUNITY: RESOURCES TO HELP OUR CITIZENS.

I fixate on the word *help*.

I take a few steps into the room to get a better look. A lot of the people are moving to the back. There's a table with a coffee urn and a stack of paper cups, the waxy kind that have foldout handles attached to the sides. Next to the cups is a plastic tray with rows of cookies. They are from the bakery, I can tell. Bottled water is arranged in two lines alongside a bunch of juice boxes. They had to have come from a variety pack, because there's super fruit punch and goodness grape. I don't think those are sold separately. I stare at the people helping themselves to the stuff, and in the middle of the group I see a flash of two small hands. One holds a cookie and the other has a juice box.

I know it's my little brother.

I start to cry.

I'm so embarrassed, I turn away and move back out into the hallway and I run right into Mrs. Hunt. I manage to say "I found him" before I feel my legs get soft. And I sink to the floor. I stare at the wall-to-wall bumpy carpeting and I see little specks of sand. It looks clean until you are on the same level, and then it's a lot dirtier than you'd think. If you get close, do you always see things differently?

I have to work hard to breathe right.

Mrs. Hunt heads into the Bromley Room and I shut my eyes.

When I open them again, she's coming out with Geno. They are talking. The cookie is gone but Geno still holds the juice box, and he's carrying a folder stuffed with brochures. He doesn't realize I'm upset. "Hey, Cordy. Are you ready to go? I found out about a bunch of community services."

"Let's give your sister a moment or two. She got worried when she couldn't find you."

Geno's face goes from happy to sad as he realizes I'm upset. He right away squats close to me. "I'm sorry, Cordy. I'm really sorry . . ."

I have to cut him off. "It's okay. I'm okay."

Only I don't think I look okay, because Mrs. Hunt says, "Let's go back to my office, kids."

We sit at a round table surrounded by books.

They are everywhere, on metal shelves and in stacks and even in messy piles that look like they could easily tip over. Up until now I didn't realize books had a smell. Maybe it's all the paper and glue and the ink. Or the plastic covers.

I see some of the books are damaged. There's a tall stack that I think were once wet and have dried out. The pages are all wavy. One cover must have been chewed up by a dog. Or maybe a teething little kid. The corners have been bitten off. I'm glad Lost doesn't do that.

I've never thought about the fact that the books leave here and have an experience in the world. The reader gets an experience with the words. But the book also has an adventure. They ride in cars and visit houses and people carry them.

I wish the books could talk.

I want to know where they've been and what they've seen and how they were treated.

I snap out of it when Mrs. Hunt says, "As you know, food isn't allowed in the library. But this room is different because it's for staff to eat in during our breaks. Cordy, you and your brother have sandwiches?"

Geno looks like he doesn't want to get into trouble. "We were going to eat them outside. On the bench. We can do that."

She interrupts him. "No, sweetheart. It's okay for you to eat in here if you're with me. It's my lunch break. Cordy, what did you bring?"

Mrs. Hunt hands me my lunch bag. I don't remember how she even got it. I take out the sandwiches Mom made. There is also a cut-up apple and chips to split. Geno still has his juice box. Mrs. Hunt gives me a bottle of water. When I finish drinking it, I'll bring it home to Lost.

Mrs. Hunt goes to a small refrigerator and comes back carrying a glass container with pasta salad. She says the noodles are called "rotini." They look like springs and are shiny, which must mean they are covered in a lot of oil. I see green olives and red peppers and chunks of cheese that has green streaks running through it. I can tell by Geno's face that he's glad we've got peanut butter sandwiches. Neither of us likes green olives or red peppers. And we've never had chunks of white cheese with green streaks. It might be rotten because it has a strong smell, but I'm not going to say anything.

It's quiet in an uncomfortable way until Mrs. Hunt says, "How about some music?" Before we can even answer, she's heading to a desk. I nod with what I hope looks like enthusiasm. I'm pretty sure she's going to have us listen to violins and pianos. It will be art music. I bet she's still thinking that would help me to calm down. But I don't feel my heart pounding anymore and I'm breathing okay.

Mrs. Hunt hits a button and the music that comes on isn't what I expect. It's a bunch of electric guitars with a lot of drumming. The singing sounds like a group of men growling. People are full of surprises.

I want to be polite, so I say, "This is a really interesting song."

"Do you like it?" She looks pleased.

I give Geno a small kick under the table and we both nod. I take a bite of my sandwich and Geno asks, "What kind of music is it, Mrs. Hunt?"

"Thrash metal. The band is Tankard. I'm in an organization called Heavy Metal Librarians."

Geno and I have no idea what she's talking about. But I suddenly wonder if she would like the book Old Mrs. Crowley gave me about the life of the record producer Clive Davis. I could offer to lend it to her, but I don't.

It would be like bringing sand to the beach.

I think she's got enough stuff to read already.

We eat our lunch and listen to the thrash metal music and I go back to letting my mind wander. It's hard to do with this racket playing in the background. When I look up, I see that Geno is already done eating and he's staring at a vending machine against the back wall that sells candy. I whisper "Dairy Queen" and he understands that there will be sweets coming our way.

It has stopped raining when we leave the library for the place Geno says is "heaven on earth." He does that to make me laugh because Old Mrs. Crowley described something called shepherd's pie that her gran made as being "heaven on earth." I have no idea what she was talking about. Her gran was from England.

I'm carrying the library books I've checked out in a gray-and-white backpack that Mrs. Hunt gave me. She said it's been in the lost and found for a long time and since no one came to claim it, it's mine now. I was so surprised. The backpack was designed to carry a computer. I don't have a computer. I wonder how the person got their computer home on the day when they left it in the library. The backpack must have been too nice to be kept in the lost and found box at the front desk, because Mrs. Hunt got it from a closet. It's the best thing I own, but having it makes me nervous. What if I'm walking home from school and a car pulls over and the driver yells at me, "Hey, kid, that's my backpack!"?

I wish I'd thought of asking Mrs. Hunt to write a note explaining she'd given it to me.

Geno is wearing a bright orange stocking cap that was in the library's lost and found box. There were gloves and scarves and notebooks and pens in there too. According to Mrs. Hunt, "the orange cap needs a new owner." Geno was happy because orange is his favorite color. We each also got to pick out a pen. Mine is red because of my hair. Geno wanted one with green ink, but there were limited options. He took a blue Sharpie. He said he's going to give it to Jose. Jose loves blue.

It's been such an up-and-down day. It started with not being able to find Lost, which scared me. Then I discovered the dolphins, and saw a pink one, which could be very lucky. But then in the library when I couldn't find my brother, I sort of lost my mind. Mrs. Hunt said she thought I might have had a "minor panic attack." She wanted to call Mom to explain, but we talked her out of it. I was okay after we found Geno and ate the sandwiches. Mom is working and doesn't need that kind of phone call.

As Geno and I walk to get our strawberry cheesecake Blizzards, the wind hits the road signs, and they make a rattling noise. Cars go by on the road and I wonder about the people inside. Where are they going and what kind of lives do they have? How many of them like pasta salad called rotini with green olives and red peppers and chunks of smelly cheese? How many of the people listen to thrash metal music from a band called Tankard? Have any of them ever seen dolphins in the Siuslaw? How many lost a parent when they were a kid?

I'm really tired when we enter Dairy Queen.

The warm air hits me hard and all I want to do is close my eyes. I give Geno money and I sit by the window with the backpack in my lap. It looks like something the McKerns from the Big House would own. It has fancy zippers and all kinds of small pockets, maybe to hold a phone.

I don't have a phone.

I put my hand in one of the side pockets and there's a piece of paper crumpled up in the bottom. It's wedged down flat and I'm guessing it has probably been there a long time.

I pull out the paper and see that it's a credit card receipt. My heart drops because I didn't have this backpack very long before I found out about the real owner. I unfold the receipt and see that it's from Fred Meyer. Everyone shops at Fred Meyer because it's so big and has so much stuff. You can buy groceries and fishing poles, but they also have a jewelry store and a bank and a pharmacy. There's a whole town in there. The receipt means the owner of my new/used backpack probably lives here, which makes sense because tourists probably don't go to our local library. The person spent $47.49 almost four months ago.

Then I see the name on the credit card receipt: *Janice Hunt*.

I know one person with the last name of Hunt, which is Mrs. Hunt from the library.

It takes me a moment to remember that Mrs. Hunt's first name is Janice. It's on her library ID, which she wears around her neck.

And then I understand: This backpack wasn't in the lost and found. That's why Mrs. Hunt went to the closet and came back with it. The librarian who likes thrash metal music and pasta salad just gave me her own backpack because she felt bad for me.

Is it because I came in and said my backpack wore out?

Is it because I lost Geno?

Is it because she knows about The Accident? Pretty much everyone has heard about what happened to Dad.

For the second time today, my eyes fill up with tears.

There is a saying that not all heroes wear capes. But I don't think *any* hero wears a cape. Real heroes wear restaurant aprons. They wear hairnets. They wear yellow fishing hats that are waterproof.

And they can wear ID cards that hang around their necks.

They have real jobs and they show up.

And because of what they do, things get better.

6.

THE NEXT MORNING, I WAKE UP EARLY.

I go outside with Lost at my heels and we head to the Big House. In the crawl space under the porch is a plastic container filled with outdoor things. There are hoses and tarps and spiders. But also, life jackets. No one has ever said we can't use this stuff. If anything is meant to be shared, it would be a flotation device.

I'd ask Mom, but she's asleep and she wouldn't want me to go down to the dock. None of the life jackets are for kids, but I take one anyway. I buckle the straps and then pull tight. It's not comfortable, but I think it's *comforting*. I'm still afraid, but if I fall into the water at least I'll be in a bright orange-and-yellow vest that will keep my head up. Plus, there's a whistle attached on a cord tucked into the right side. I'm not sure who would hear it, but I'm not going to question a safety feature.

When I get to the dock, there are no dolphins. Lost stares out at the moving water. He doesn't bark. It's cold and patchy fog hangs in places, making the riverbank on the other side seem very far away. The wind picks up and the fog moves toward us, and so does sand. It lifts into the air and stings my face. I'm afraid to be down here, but I want to see the dolphins, so I have to push the fear to the back of my mind.

The sky in all directions is gray and lumpy with clouds.

There is a chance of rain.

There is always a chance of rain.

Except for six weeks in the summer, there is a very good chance of rain.

I sit down on the dock and wait. I try not to be worried about the water. I know that two opposite things can happen at the same time. This was hard for me to understand when I was younger. Like right now the river is loud because of the rushing water, but the world around me feels very quiet. There aren't man-made sounds. No cars or trucks or planes or boats.

After a while, the river's sound disappears because it's so constant.

What's left is the wind and the wild.

Lost, in a crouch at my side, has his chin raised and his tail in a tight curl. He's on high alert with his little ears. Maybe he's also hoping the pod will return. I read in one of my library books that scientists who study dolphins have figured out that a pod is constantly changing. A dolphin can be in one group and then switch to another. A pod can be as few as two dolphins, or as many as twenty. Different pods can join together, and then just as easily come apart.

Dolphin pods make me think about school and friend groups, which also aren't set.

After The Accident I was so lucky to have Button. But she is taking her swimming more seriously now. I sometimes go with her to practice. I don't mind sitting and watching. It gives me time to think. It means I don't have to pretend or explain if I'm sad. Mom says it's okay for me to need "more space." Now that I have Lost waiting at home, he takes away some of the sadness. That might be why people live with animals. There's another beating heart close by. Maybe you can't hear it, but you feel it.

Comfort means different things to different people.

Mrs. Hunt gets comfort from a thrash metal band.

Old Mrs. Crowley gets it from reading about a record producer named Clive Davis.

Geno gets comfort from being with his friend Jose, looking for hidden treasure, and having Dairy Queen Blizzards.

Mom gets it from watching episodes of an old show called *Friends* and going to bed early.

I get comfort from a little dog with very bad breath. And we're right now together, staring out at a roaring river as it heads into the ocean. There aren't dolphins today, but there is still so much to see.

I hear my name and turn to find Geno. He's heading down the path to the dock. He's got on jeans, but the top from his Halloween costume, which was Maui from the movie *Moana*. He loves that character. He's is carrying a paper sack, and he calls out, "I've been looking all over for you! I baked us cinnamon bread."

Geno reaches into the brown bag. He has taken plain bread, toasted it, and then put on butter sprinkled with sugar and cinnamon. He thinks that makes him a baker. I don't correct him. I just say "Thanks, Bud."

He heads down the dock and sits next to me to eat. He talks while he chews. "How come you're down here? Is that life jacket from the McKerns'? Is it because you're scared of the water?"

I nod. He keeps going. "We wore life jackets when we went out on Dad's boat. Mom always says to stay off the dock."

I'm not sure what to tell him, but I go with the truth. "I saw dolphins yesterday and I thought they might come back."

"You saw dolphins in the river?" His voice is excited. I'm glad he realizes that it's a big deal.

"Yeah. And there were a lot of them."

"I've never seen a dolphin in the river."

"Me neither. Until yesterday."

"Should we save part of the toast to feed them—if they show up?"

"No, Geno. We're not supposed to do that. It's bad to feed wild animals. It changes their habits."

He mumbles, "Oh. Sorry."

I didn't mean to sound like I was lecturing him, but somehow it came out that way. I can see a change in my little brother's face. I feel bad. "I'd love for us to feed them. But I know it's not right."

The life jacket is big and bulky, but I put my arm around my little brother. Geno gets over stuff quickly. He goes from looking sad to happy, and takes another bite of his toast. I wonder if I should tell him about the pink dolphin. I'm still thinking about it when a seagull soars low overhead. Maybe it sees the cinnamon toast. I remember something Dad said about gulls. I try to share stuff I know about the world with Geno, because Dad always did that for me.

"Geno, did you know seagulls are one of the few birds that can drink fresh water *and* salt water?"

"The salt doesn't make them sick?"

"They get rid of it. They have glands close to their eyes. The salt goes down a tube and comes out a hole in their nose."

"Out their beak?"

"Yeah. The beak."

Geno gives me a look like he doesn't believe me. "Cordy, is that for real?"

"Things in nature are way more interesting than anything I could make up."

Geno doesn't seem convinced.

The wind is blowing in gusts, bending the silverweed, which grows in clumps along the river, until it's nearly flat. Our little dog takes off, leaving the dock and heading back to the large rocks. There are a dozen sandpipers there and Lost likes to make their lives miserable.

"Cordy, can you see the gland?"

"What gland?"

"In the seagulls."

"No. It's under the feathers, under their skin. A bird's feathers are like our hair."

"So their skin is like our scalp?"

"Yeah."

"Do dolphins have skin?"

"Yeah. I read it's twenty times thicker than ours."

"How much thicker is a cow's skin from our skin?"

"I don't know. I was only reading about dolphins."

Geno keeps chewing, then he has a thought. "At school Mrs. Mason said that it's important to have thick skin."

"She means not to let people upset you."

"I don't let people upset me."

I think about what he just said. Geno doesn't pay attention to most negative stuff. He's special that way.

I want to have thick skin.

I'm wondering how to go about doing that when Geno shouts, "A bald eagle!"

It doesn't matter how many times you've seen a bald eagle, it always feels important.

Geno and I watch as the bird glides down from up high to soar low over the middle of the river. His wing span is so big. I'm hoping that he catches a fish, but he doesn't. Instead, he flaps his strong wings and rises back up. His eyes look so focused, but I don't think he sees us. Geno whispers, "Cordy, tell me again why they call them bald? He's got feathers."

I've told him before, but he's not obsessed like me with where words come from. "It's because the word *balde* a long time ago in Old English meant 'white.' So people back then were calling them white eagles, because of the white feathers on their heads. But the meaning of the word changed."

Geno leans close, his voice soft. "What's another word like that? One that changed?"

I have to think, but I come up with an answer. "*Awful*. A long time ago it meant 'full of awe.' So it was good. Like *successful* means 'full of success.'"

"I wonder how that happens. A word changing. Especially to something that's the opposite. Poor bald eagles got stuck with a bad name."

"Yeah. Like Old Mrs. Crowley. Only she probably doesn't know that's what everyone calls her."

"I guess the bald eagles don't know either."

The eagle swings around and glides toward us. He makes four sharp, high-pitched whistles. It isn't what you'd think would come out of a bird that size.

Geno says exactly what I'm thinking. "I feel like an eagle should sound more powerful."

"Maybe a bald eagle doesn't have to be fierce because it knows it's in charge."

I can see that Geno likes this idea. "Yeah, they really call the shots." Suddenly he looks worried. "We should get Lost over here."

He's right. Lost has a loud bark, but he's a little dog. We both stand up and start shouting his name.

It's one of those times that I'm glad no one is around to hear us. Lost lifts his head when we call him and comes running. He learned his name so quickly. He's a genius dog.

Until we started yelling, the eagle didn't seem to notice us. Eagles don't like people very much and they keep away. Now that we're on our feet calling for our dog, the large bird watches. Or is he actually focused on our dog?

Lost scrambles down the dock right into my arms. I hold him tight. The eagle changes direction and heads back up the river. I release Lost from my firm grip. I guess he smells the cinnamon toast, because he tries to lick my face. I probably have sugar in the corners of my mouth.

"Lost, stop it!" I try to calm him down, but it doesn't work. He only gets more excited. This makes Geno laugh.

"He loves you, Cordy. He can't help himself."

I'm laughing now too. "He's got the worst breath. Maybe he ate a dead fish or something."

"No. Lost always has that smell. You just have to decide it's not bad."

I'm not sure how you do that, but maybe it's like the boathouse. Half the time I forget about the long-gone fishing nets, but they're still in the air. I think Geno might be right. So much stuff is how you choose to see it. Or smell it.

I like to think I'm the one teaching Geno, because he's so much younger than me. But I'm wrong. He has his own way of viewing life. And he laughs so easily. Listening to him do that might be my favorite thing in the world right now.

We stay on the dock waiting for dolphins until it starts to rain. At first, we don't care, but then Lost has had enough. He shakes, and water flies into our faces.

It's time to go back to the boathouse.

7.

I DECIDE LOST NEEDS TO GO TO THE VET.

I read that bad breath could mean a dog has something seriously wrong with their health. I can't stop worrying about it. I would be a bad pet owner to ignore a real problem.

At dinner time I make a cheese omelet for Geno and me. I'll serve it with Tater Tots. I take two handfuls out of a freezer bag. It says they need twenty to twenty-four minutes in the oven, but that's a lie. We eat them all the time after only being cooked for twelve minutes, because we can't wait any longer. They're cold in the middle, but we've had them that way for so long, Geno thinks that's how a Tater Tot is supposed to be served.

It goes to show you that the food you like might just be the food you're used to.

While we're eating, Geno asks, "What are you thinking about?"

"I want Lost to see a doctor."

"Does that cost a bunch of money?"

I nod. "I'm afraid to tell Mom because we haven't had him that long. We all love him. But she might think it's a UE."

Geno knows about UEs. "I don't think it's an unnecessary expense. Lost is necessary."

"I know. But it's like she says, 'We have to run a tight ship.'"

Geno swallows a Tator Tot and then goes to the little table by the front door where all kinds of things are stacked. Mail and free magazines are piled alongside empty bags to take to the market. Geno looks through the mess and comes back with his folder from the library.

"There's a free animal clinic in town." He takes a brochure from the folder. He starts reading. "The county helps underwrite a . . ."

He stops. He's stuck on a word. I look over. "Dedicated."

Geno hands me the brochure. "Can you read it?"

"The county helps underwrite a dedicated group of animal professionals available to provide services for low-income members of our community."

Geno suddenly remembers another thing they said. "It's called pro bone service."

"Pro bono. That means 'for the public good.'"

"How do you know that?"

"It's from Latin. I like words."

"Cordy, keep reading the brochure."

"The first Wednesday of every month a clinic is held at the humane society."

"Not the human society."

"No. *Human* is a person. The humane society is for animals that need help. "

"Shouldn't it be called the pet society?"

I keep reading. "Pet care is provided on a first come, first served basis. No appointment necessary, starting at twelve p.m."

Lost has his head on Geno's foot. He's dozing until it's time to lick our plates. Geno looks excited. "This Wednesday is the first of the month! Maybe Mom can take him to see the doctor."

"Mom works Wednesdays. She won't miss a shift. She's saving her money."

"We can ask."

"No. I'll figure it out."

"How?"

"I'll talk to her about letting me go. You did a good thing bringing that folder home."

Geno smiles. "Thanks. Plus, I got free cookies and a juice box."

"I promise I'll get something worked out." I stare down at the floor. "Okay, Lost?"

Our dog's eyes stay closed but his ears lift at the sound of his name. Geno goes back to his Tater Tots. When I say I have something covered, he knows I mean it.

Being a big sister comes with a lot of power. I try to use it in a good way.

I start thinking of how to get Lost to the free appointment. I could pretend to be sick and stay home, then walk him to the humane society. It's not that far. I take long walks all the time. But this town is so small. Someone might see me and then tell Mom. Also, if I say I'm sick, what if one of the parents from school drives by and wonders why I'm not home? They could rat me out to a teacher. It's important to tell the truth, especially when there's a really good chance you'll get caught if you don't.

I decide to wait to talk to Mom about it. I don't want to give her a lot of time to think through the situation. On Tuesday, as soon as she comes home from work, I explain that the next day I could take Lost to get a free checkup. I give her Geno's brochure. Mom is quiet as she reads. When she's done, she puts it down. I can tell she's not going for it. "I have work tomorrow, so I can't take him."

I was expecting this. "Mom, I know. I don't want you to miss work. I can do it. This is more important than one day of school."

"Cordy—"

I interrupt her because I'm building my case, and it's

good to keep going if you're trying to win an argument. "I'll get my homework from other kids. I have only two absences so far and it's almost the end of the school year."

Every June at a big assembly they give awards to the kids who have perfect attendance. I was in the running for that until March, when I had a sweaty fever and Mom made me stay home. You only get a certificate for never missing one single day. It's not a gift card or something worth the effort of going to school sick, which is what Lena Furtick does. She says she doesn't care about the awards, though. The reason she shows up is because she's in the free breakfast and lunch program and she's hungry at home. Lena has her priorities in the right place.

I've gone over what to say to Mom and I'm prepared. "I read that bad breath in a dog can mean real problems. It's not responsible of us to let it go. We need to do something and this is an amazing chance because Geno found the free doctor."

I look over at Lost. He's lying down and his eyes are closed, but one of his ears is facing forward. He's only half asleep.

Mom sighs. I know this is the first step to her possibly giving in. "Cordy, tomorrow we have a big group coming in for lunch for Len Zolezzi's birthday. And Angie's going to be eating with them, not working the floor, since she's Len's half sister. So we're already short-staffed."

"Mom, I can take Lost on my *own*. That's what I've

been saying. I'll be fine." I think of another point. "Also, it would be sort of a school assignment because I need to come up with one more thing for the real-life skills checklist that shows how I took responsibility. Ross Ledbetter used the fact that he fed his sister's guinea pigs when she got in her bike crash. So pet stuff totally works."

I can see Mom thinking. I hope it's not about Ross Ledbetter's sister, who broke her leg when someone in a parked car opened the door right into the bike lane. Jesse Ledbetter couldn't stop in time. It was a bad accident. I saw a picture of her on the ground after she had just thrown up.

Mom says, "Cordy, I know you're responsible enough. But I'm not sure someone your age can bring in a dog without an adult."

"It doesn't say anything about that in the brochure." Then I go in a different direction. "Mom, I'll explain that you wanted to be there. But the clinic is only one day a month and you're a single parent and you have to work. I bet that would for sure mean we'd get the exam for free."

This makes Mom laugh. It wasn't supposed to be funny, but anytime she can laugh is a good thing. I can see that I'm starting to get somewhere when she picks up the brochure and looks at it again. After a few moments she says, "I could give you my cell phone. You and Lost would walk to the humane society. Then you could call the restaurant and let me talk to the doctor."

"A licensed veterinarian. That's what it says. You could even FaceTime if you want to see the person."

"I don't need to FaceTime. You'll just call the restaurant."

I nod. She has a plan. And I do too, because it was my plan.

I go over to Lost and lift him up off the floor. I hold my sweet dog over my shoulder like I'm burping a baby. His head is close and his breath is pretty terrible. Only I'm not going to worry about that because we're going to see a veterinarian. Maybe Lost just needs special chewy bones. I whisper to him, "You and me. Me and you. And maybe a breath mint or two." I'd make it into a song, but I'm not singing these days.

In the morning, Mom gets really nervous at breakfast because she's going to be without her cell phone. She says it feels like she's missing an arm. I think that's really exaggerating, but I nod as if I understand, even though I don't have a phone like most of the kids my age. I say that she can borrow Angie's phone or Tommy's or use the phone in the restaurant and call me as many times as she wants. Then Geno asks if he can miss school and go with me to the "dog doctor."

Mom says "a hard no" to that idea.

I'm happy when they both leave and it's just me and Lost.

I put in a load of laundry and give Lost a bath in the

sink using dishwashing liquid, not Mom's shampoo because she says not to waste it on a dog. I dry him off as much as I can and then place him in the laundry basket with a heater in front of him. He's not very happy, but I bet it feels special that he's not home alone today. I sit down and look at the brochure about the low-income veterinary clinic. I've already read it a bunch of times. But if I get anxious about something, I read the instructions over more than once. It helps.

I decide to straighten up and put things away. Mom will be happy about this. When I move the mail by the front door, I see one of Mom's to-do lists. It says:

- *Check to see if the kids need new shoes.*
- *Buy vacuum cleaner bags.*
- *Find out if the septic tank should be pumped.*
- *Get out of this little town and start a new life!*

I stare at number four. I don't think it's something that should be on a to-do list. I put the paper back in the pile of stuff, and go to the worst kitchen in the world and drink the leftover coffee. I'm not supposed to do this, but it's what's called an act of defiance. I tell myself that getting out of this town and starting a new life is not as easy as buying vacuum cleaner bags.

When it's time to leave for the humane society, I put Lost's new harness over his head and snap it around his belly. He looks very confused. He's only had to wear this thing once when we went over to Mom's friend Gigi's house. Gigi has a lot of cats and she wanted to meet Lost but was worried that he might be a cat hater. He isn't.

Lost blinks a bunch of times and his tail tucks between his legs. I can see he's anxious. Maybe he has bad memories from the past with a harness. I try to reassure him. "You're not going to a bad place." He looks like he understands, but of course he doesn't. Lost has an empty plastic water bottle that he sleeps next to on my bed. I go get it. It's his lovey.

It stops raining just as we are leaving, but the wind is still strong. Lost pulls on the leash, maybe trying to show me that he's healthy and strong. He can have a real attitude.

The humane society is farther than I thought, but we arrive almost thirty minutes early. I'd always rather get somewhere ahead of time than be late. From a distance I can hear the sound of barking dogs. I reach the door right behind a man who holds a case with a handle. It's like a fishing tackle box, only it's made of leather. I'm pretty sure no one would have a fishing tackle box made out of leather, because the first time it got wet it would be ruined. Maybe it's luggage. Or maybe there's an animal inside, but I don't think so because there aren't any holes for breathing.

The man waits, holding the door open for me. But Lost

stops. He won't go in, even when I pull hard on the leash. Maybe the barking dogs are trying to warn him. Finally, I pick up Lost and carry him under my arm. I bet I look like a bad pet owner. The man with the leather bag is nice because he doesn't get irritated waiting. I wonder where his sick pet is. The man is wearing jeans and a big puffy coat. His hair is black and his eyes are dark brown. He has a mustache that is very well trimmed. Albert Einstein, who was my famous person to learn about last year, also had a mustache, but his was not well trimmed.

Once we are inside, the man says good morning to the woman behind the counter. I'm guessing he might have come to Florence from Eugene, because she asks about his drive and he says it was good, just over an hour. Then he heads through a door that says *Staff Only*.

So now it's just me and the woman. I'm suddenly nervous and I feel like I'm losing my voice. The woman has to ask me three times for my name. "Is your mom or dad with you? Are they parking the car?"

I shake my head. The woman looks concerned. Maybe you do have to be a certain age to take an animal to the free clinic. I manage to say, "My mom couldn't get off work, so I'm bringing in our dog. I'm supposed to call her from here."

The woman doesn't like this answer, but then another woman comes out who looks familiar. I've seen her before by the boat ramp under the river. I don't know her name, but I guess she realizes who I am, because she takes charge and starts to put papers on a clipboard. The other woman sighs and says, "Can you tell me your dog's name?"

I suddenly wish he wasn't called Lost, but it's too late to do anything about that. I say very clearly, "His name is Lost."

People can be crummy listeners. She says, "So he's lost?"

I shake my head and I can feel my confidence slipping. I wish I'd brought my new gray-and-white backpack. I feel better when I'm carrying it. I manage to say, "No. That's just his name."

The second woman is back in charge. She hands me the clipboard and says I should answer the questions as best as I can. She doesn't dwell on the name problem.

I try to fill out the form but I don't know the answers to half the questions.

- *Who is your employer?*
- *What is your marital status? Single? Married? Divorced? Widowed?*
- *If married, what is your spouse's name?*
- *Who is your spouse's employer?*
- *Do you currently qualify for food stamps or other government assistance?*
- *How old is your pet?*

- *What is your pet's breed?*
- *When was the last time your pet saw a veterinarian?*
- *What vaccinations has your pet previously had?*
- *Is your pet neutered or intact or spayed?*

I think I should go.

Lost does too. He pulls as hard as he can toward the front door. The clipboard falls out of my hands and hits the floor. The pages come off and I see the last page was a release form. I'm a minor so I wouldn't have been able to sign it anyway.

I feel like I am learning some "real-life skills." I'm also learning that no one trusts a kid.

8.

THE WOMAN BEHIND THE COUNTER STOPS ME FROM leaving.

The other one, who I recognize from the boat ramp, says that I can fill out the paperwork later. She says I'm early but the doctor is early too, so he can take a look at my dog right away. Lost turns toward her and he doesn't snarl at her, but it's pretty close. His upper lip curls back and I can see his little front teeth, which are brown and stained. His tail is tucked under his body.

We both want out.

But instead of heading for the door, I do my best to lead Lost through the staff-only entrance back to the exam room. Lost's acting like he's never met me, so I have to pick him up again. Just then, the door opens in the hallway and I see the same guy who came in with me. He's now wearing a white coat with a name tag that says Dr. Mazari. So this guy is one of the *"dedicated group of animal professionals available to provide services for low-income members of our community."*

He says, "We meet again."

I nod. Even though we haven't met.

He smiles. I notice he has really good teeth. He says, "I'm the veterinarian who will be looking at your dog today. I'm Dr. Mazari."

I should say, "I'm Cordy Jenkins." But I'm speechless, which my parents would say is not polite. Dr. Mazari opens a glass door to a room that has two chairs, and he motions to one. I see his luggage is open and there is medicine and other supplies inside. The veterinarian takes the clipboard from the woman and I manage to say, "My mom is at work at Curly's Seafood, where she's a waitress and she couldn't get out of today's shift because it's Len Zolezzi's birthday, but she's ready for us to call her."

"Curly's has great clam chowder," he says.

"If you like clam chowder." I don't know why I just said that. But it makes Dr. Mazari smile.

"Yes. And you aren't a fan?"

"I'd rather have chicken noodle. But they don't make it."

"My favorite soup is lentil."

I feel better because we just made a soup connection. It's something.

Dr. Mazari leans down close to Lost, who doesn't look like a fan of soup or of anyone in this building. His ears are back against his head and his eyes are wide and they aren't blinking. "Let's get this little fellow up and take a look at him."

I think he means for me to do this but before Lost or I know what's happening, Dr. Mazari scoops up my dog and sets him down on the table. The doctor's got his full attention now.

"You're here because of your dog's halitosis."

I correct him. "I'm here because he has really bad breath."

Dr. Mazari smiles. He has a stethoscope and he presses the end onto the left side of Lost's body, behind his front leg. He's listening, so I stay quiet. Then he uses a small light to look into Lost's ears. And then his eyes. He takes a few tugs on his fur. I'm glad I gave him a bath. He examines all four of Lost's paws, and then looks at his tail and his bottom. But he still hasn't even had a peek into Lost's mouth, which is where the problem is. I don't say anything about the fact that he's checking out the wrong places.

Finally, he's ready to do some actual work.

Dr. Mazari says, "When I examine your sweet dog's mouth, I'm going to be looking for brown stains, which is tartar buildup, and then for gingivitis, which means a problem with the gums. They should be pink."

I like that he understands that Lost is sweet.

I feel like I should call Mom, but things are moving quickly. There's a light on a bendable arm and Dr. Mazari aims it at Lost's head and then turns it on. It's bright. He holds Lost's jaw with one hand and sticks two fingers inside his mouth with the other. I'm trying not to freak out because I'm sure that Lost is going to bite the guy.

Luckily, he doesn't. I guess he knows he's dealing with a professional. Lost makes a small yip. I've been sitting but I can't stop myself from jumping up. Dr. Mazari says in a soft voice, "It's okay, Lost. You're good."

I see that Lost's back legs start to shake.

And then Dr. Mazari is done.

He lifts Lost off the table and sets him on the floor. He looks at me. "I'm glad you brought him in."

Dr. Mazari tells me that Lost has four, maybe five, rotten teeth. They are loose in the back of his mouth and they need to come out. The bad teeth have made Lost's gums really infected. Poor Lost. He has to be in pain. No wonder he will *carry* sticks, but never chew them. Dr. Mazari says, "We need to take care of this sweet little guy as soon as possible." I start to feel dizzy when I hear the bad teeth news.

The woman from the dock leads me back down the hallway. I have Lost on his leash. There is a woman with a pet carrier in the waiting room. Inside is a cat with only one eye. Across from her are a man and woman who are sitting together. The man holds a tiny dog who has to be very old. His face is gray and his eyes have a white layer over them. I take a seat next to the one-eyed cat and wait, because I'm going to be given a written report of today's exam. Fortunately, Lost is not interested in the cat or the old dog.

He's traumatized from the doctor visit.

I'm traumatized too.

We're not in the blue plastic chair for very long before the woman comes out from behind the counter to give me the record of "the doctor's findings." She starts by handing me a small green plastic bottle, which she says has "antibiotics Lost needs to start immediately." They are prescription, but she says there won't be any charge. She tells me to make sure to have my mom read the instructions. I put the bottle of pills in my coat pocket.

Then she hands me an envelope and I'm not sure if I'm supposed to look at it at home, or open it here. But I do it right now because maybe Mom will have questions. I realize I haven't called her. I take out the two pieces of paper and the first thing I see is that Dr. Mazari is recommending that Lost have dental surgery immediately. They don't do that kind of stuff here. He has made a referral to three different veterinarians in Florence who can do the procedure.

The next part is the shocker.

There is an estimate of what we can expect to pay. Taking out Lost's crummy teeth means he has to be put under anesthesia! It's surgery. I read, "We estimate that a reputable doctor would charge between $1,200 and $2,500, depending on how many teeth will need extraction."

I can't believe how much it's going to cost! We can't afford something that expensive. But Lost is in pain. He could die early because of his rotten teeth. The doctor said his gums are infected and that could spread. I stare at the piece of paper and the words get all wobbly and I realize that my eyes have filled with tears.

I will not cry.

I will not cry in a public place in front of the lady with the one-eyed cat and the couple with the really old gray dog.

But I can't stop myself.

I want to get up and run out, but my legs don't work. I'm frozen in this chair and my feet feel like concrete. Lost is on my lap and he looks up and starts licking my tears. I love him. I remember what Geno said about changing how you feel about bad smells. Suddenly, Lost's stinky breath smells fine.

The next thing I know, I'm back in the examining room. The woman from the dock is holding a glass of water and telling me to breathe. Then the door opens and Dr. Mazari comes in. His voice is soft. "Can you tell us what's wrong?"

I manage to say, "It's too much money. We won't be able to do it."

Dr. Mazari says, "Cordy, I don't want you to worry.

We're going to take care of Lost." He remembered our names. I don't think I ever told him mine, but it was one of the only things I filled out on the form. I try to nod but I can't because I'm concentrating on not crying. Suddenly all I can think about is losing Dad, which doesn't have anything to do with the bill to have Lost's teeth pulled, only maybe it does.

Dr. Mazari says he wants to call my mom.

The woman takes my phone. I hear her voice but I'm not looking at her. Everyone in this town knows about us. She calls Curly's Seafood and asks to speak with Casey Jenkins. It doesn't take very long before I hear my mom's voice coming out of the speaker. "Hello?"

"Casey, it's Daria Obermeier. I'm calling from the humane society."

Mom sounds really far away. "Is everything okay there? I'm so sorry I couldn't come in today."

Daria Obermeier interrupts her. "Yes, your daughter is fine and her little dog is here and got his diagnosis. I'm going to put on Dr. Mazari." She hands the phone to the doctor. He looks over at me and then he begins to speak. His voice is very calm. "This is Dr. Mazari from the clinic. I've examined your dog, and he's going to need dental surgery."

I hear Mom's voice. "Oh, no."

Dr. Mazari continues talking. "It's expensive, but I have an idea how we can get around the cost."

My eyes feel all watery, so I stare at the floor.

"Oregon State University has a veterinary program and I teach there once a week. I'm thinking that if your dog's procedure could be observed by students, we might be able to do it for no charge."

I look up at the doctor. He keeps talking. He's explaining more things. Lost is staring up at him too. Did the vet say the words "no charge"?

Did Lost hear the words "dental surgery"?

Dr. Mazari ends the call. He hands the phone back to me. "Your mom is going to come get you." I nod and he smiles. "She just needs to finish serving Len Zolezzi's birthday cake."

Lost and I wait in the staff-only area. It's like being in the library where Mrs. Hunt let us eat lunch. It's an off-limits place to the public. The chairs in here are way more comfortable than out front and it's very quiet.

I'm starting to feel better. I don't want to tell anyone that earlier I drank coffee. It might be a contributing factor to why I feel so jumpy.

Daria comes in and gives me a packet of orange-colored crackers that have peanut butter inside. She also brings in a bottle of apple juice and a little dish of water for Lost. He must be freaked out, because he doesn't drink anything and he's not begging for my crackers.

Once I've calmed down, I realize what an interesting

place this is. The walls have framed pictures of animals with sayings underneath. "Foster a Dog Today" and "Rescue a Pet–Change Two Lives." The poster I like best has a dog who looks like it's smiling. The caption says: "All You Need Is a Friend."

When I'm old enough I wonder if I can volunteer here. I could walk the dogs or do other chores. I bet Geno would like that too.

Daria comes to check on me and decides to "prop open the door to get more air in here."

I don't need more air, but I'm glad she's opened the door because now I can see into the examining room.

I watch Dr. Mazari give eye drops to the cat, who I find out is named Sinbad. The old dog named Fred gets a shot to help his arthritis. The doctor then examines a rabbit that arrives in a basket, and after that a woman brings in a bird. I hear her tell Daria that it has "wet nostrils and diarrhea."

I feel like all birds have diarrhea, but I guess not.

Also, I didn't know they had nostrils.

Once the bird leaves, Dr. Mazari and Daria come in and sit with me. But Daria doesn't stay long because someone is at the front with a box of kittens that have been "surrendered." I'd like to see them but I don't ask if I can because I'm afraid I'll fall in love with one and I know Mom will say we're not getting a cat.

We have enough pet problems right now.

Dr. Mazari opens his computer and begins typing. He is updating the files on the "patients" he saw today.

I say to him, "You have a really interesting job."

"I think so." He smiles.

I find myself asking, "Do you know anything about ocean animals?"

"I've had aquatic animal training."

"Have you seen very many albino ocean animals?"

"No. I haven't been lucky enough to have that happen."

I tell him, "I saw an albino dolphin in the Siuslaw with its pod. It felt pretty special."

Dr. Mazari looks impressed. "An albino dolphin would be a very rare sighting."

"It was pink. And pretty small. Up until today I thought it might be good luck."

"It's interesting, the idea of luck. It helps explain things. We're always looking for that, right? For why things happen."

"Mom says we have to stop saying 'Why did this happen to us?' And change to 'What're we going to do about it?' I don't think she came up with that herself. I think she read it somewhere."

"It's still great."

"We only got Lost last month. He was on the street. I think he was abandoned. Maybe somebody didn't have the money to fix his rotten teeth. Maybe that's why he was out wandering around in the rain by himself."

"You know who's lucky? Your sweet little dog to have found you."

I pick up Lost and hold him in my lap.

I'm the lucky one, but I don't say that.

9.

MOM SHOWS UP TO GET ME.

She must have been in a real hurry, because she walks in wearing her orange work apron, which is embarrassing. I'm just glad she doesn't have on the *Keep Clam and Carry On* hat. She's carrying two restaurant sacks with take-out containers inside. She has a Bay Shrimp Louie Salad and Curly's Seafood Alfredo, which is noodles with salmon, cod, and shrimp. They are for Dr. Mazari and Daria Obermeier. Mom didn't realize there was another woman at the front counter, so I guess they'll have to share. She also brought marionberry cobbler and a piece of peanut butter pie.

She doesn't get this stuff free; she pays half price. I bet they don't know. I want to tell them, but I don't want to be pushy.

Geno and I get a slice of peanut butter pie only if it's a special day.

Lost goes crazy when he sees Mom. He can't stop jumping and spinning in the air. He lands hard a bunch of times on the black-and-white linoleum floor. I'm worried he's going to hurt himself, then I realize there's an animal doctor here, so at least he'd get medical care right away. I think Lost just wants Mom to get him out of this place, only it comes off looking like she's the most loved dog owner on the planet.

I'm proud of him. He knows when to turn it on at the right time.

Dr. Mazari seems really happy about the Seafood Alfredo and also the slice of peanut butter pie. He says he doesn't usually eat until he leaves, which is sometimes not till four o'clock. He thanks Mom a bunch of times and she keeps thanking him back. It's one big thank-you conversation. They finally stop when Daria Obermeier gives Mom the clipboard with the paperwork I didn't fill out. I'm told to take Lost and wait in the car because more dogs are coming in and I guess we're in the way.

Lost is as happy to leave as I've ever seen him. Once we are outside, he pees on a pole that looks like it's been used by every dog who's ever left this place. The grass and weeds around the area are dead and the pole is rusty for the bottom two feet. I bet the dogs think just getting out of the building is an achievement and should be marked. I think for a dog, lifting a leg is the same as signing their name.

Lost scratches the ground once he's done, sending dirt and weeds flying. I have to pull him hard to make him stop. Dogs have glands between their toes and they claw on the ground to leave even more of their special scent.

I read that humans used to have a better sense of smell than we do today, but over time eyesight became important. I think I'd rather *see* the world than smell it, for a lot of reasons.

We get inside the truck and Lost climbs into my lap.

I kiss the top of his head. We did it.

Although the doors and windows are closed, I can still hear the sound of the breeze in the pine trees. Today went well because Lost is going to get his crummy mouth fixed and it's not going to cost us a ton of money. I feel like singing. I don't, but still, it's nice to want to.

I wait for what seems like a long time.

Finally, I turn around and look back at the building, and through the glass doors I see Dr. Mazari in the waiting area talking to Mom. I wonder if he has something new to tell her.

After a lot more talking, Dr. Mazari takes out a cell phone from the back pocket of his jeans. It looks like he's putting in Mom's number. She then does the same thing. I guess he's going to contact her about the plan for Lost's free teeth-pulling.

Mom comes out and gets into the truck. She looks down at her lap and says, "I can't believe I've had on my work apron this whole time."

"I was going to tell you, but it was awkward."

Mom laughs. She's in a really good mood. She says, "What a nice man!"

"Dr. Mazari?"

"Yes. He seems like a really good guy."

"Yeah. And how about Lost? He's got big problems. It's a good thing we got him in to see a doctor!"

"I'll say. You made all this happen! I'm so proud of you, Cordy."

"Thanks. Geno played a big part too."

I'm thinking she might not have been so proud if she saw me crying in there, and also, if she knew I drank the leftover coffee back at home. I ask, "So what are the next steps for Lost?"

He's asleep with his head hanging over my legs and his nose pushing right into the seat. He passed out as soon as he got into the truck. I'm guessing the two hours in that place were really stressful. But now he opens his eyes and looks at Mom.

"Taj is going to check with the university and then let me know as soon as he can."

"Taj?"

"Dr. Mazari. He said to call him Taj."

"I've never heard of someone named Taj."

"His parents are from Pakistan."

"When did he say that?"

"When I was talking to him just now."

"Oh. No wonder it took so long. He was giving you his life story."

I sound bratty, which no one likes, but I'm annoyed that she was learning all these facts about the veterinarian's parents when I was sitting out here waiting. But Mom doesn't get mad. She laughs.

"I didn't hear his life story. Just that his mom and dad were born in Pakistan. And he was born in Houston."

"Texas?"

"Yeah."

"They speak Urdu in Pakistan. I wonder if he's bilingual. I wish I was bilingual. Probably not with Urdu, because I wouldn't get to use it very much, but any second language would be good to know."

"Cordy, I'm always impressed with the stuff you're interested in."

Normally that would make me feel good, but instead I'm wondering what other things Dr. Mazari told her. It seems like this guy is a real blabbermouth. I'm feeling all jumpy, and I don't think it's because of the coffee.

"What else were you guys talking about?"

"He went over what we'll need to do before Lost has his teeth pulled. He won't be able to eat after midnight the night before. That kind of thing."

All I can say is "Okay."

She adds, "Also, we'll have to get to OSU really early the morning of his surgery. And we won't be able to take Lost home until the end of the day."

"What's OSU?"

"Oregon State University. In Corvallis. Where we'll meet Taj."

"I thought he was from Eugene."

"He lives in Eugene, but he works one day a week at the university in Corvallis. It's not far. The University of Oregon in Eugene doesn't have a veterinary school."

Anytime I hear talk about the town of Eugene, I get irritated. "Those are both really boring places," I say.

Mom laughs. What I said wasn't funny. Why is she laughing? She says, "Honey, I think most people think Florence is pretty boring."

"Those are people who don't know what we have here."

Mom swings the truck out of the parking lot. "Taj said you were a great kid. And were interested in animals."

"That's all he said?" I can't stop myself. Maybe he told Mom about the dolphins in the river. "I mean–nothing else about me?"

"He did ask me a funny question about you."

"What was that?"

"He asked me if you were a 'reliable narrator.'"

"What's that supposed to mean?" I'm outraged. I don't even try to hide it.

Mom laughs again. She's not outraged. "I asked the same thing!"

"How did he answer?"

"He said what he meant was whether you make up stuff."

"What did you tell him?"

"I said, 'No. Cordy tells it like she sees it.'"

I'm happy with Mom's answer, but so mad at myself. Does Dr. Mazari, also known to some people as Taj, think I lied about seeing dolphins in the river? I bet he doesn't believe that I saw an albino dolphin!

Then I have a new thought: It might be a *good* thing if he thinks I'm someone who goes around pretending to see pink animals. It's like I have imaginary friends. In a lot of TV shows, movies, and even books, the kid with red hair is trouble. Maybe he's been affected by that. Those things can create bias. Mrs. Bingham said we were going to study that if we had time this year, but so far there haven't been any bias discussions.

Mom puts on the turn signal and pulls onto New Hope Lane. She's still smiling. I realize since The Accident I'm not used to seeing her face this way. She says, "I'm glad I brought the food. Taj seemed really happy about it."

"Who doesn't like a piece of peanut butter pie from Curly's? It's my favorite. What's your favorite pie?"

She doesn't answer me.

I can see she's thinking about something else.

I go down to the river when we get home, but there are no dolphins. I don't wait around for very long. I'm tired from today and I need to see what assignments I missed at school. Once I'm back, Mom drives to the market and returns with our regular groceries, but also a rotisserie chicken. She doesn't want to give Lost his dry dog food for dinner now that she knows his teeth are hurting. He's like Pierre in the Big House! He gets chicken cut up into little pieces with a scoop of warm rice mixed in. Mom's really babying "her little boy." Before, I was the one who treated him the most like a full family member. Interesting.

While Mom starts to cook dinner, Geno comes home from Jose's and he wants to hear about the visit to the doctor. I'm about to explain what happened, but Mom jumps in before I can speak.

"The veterinarian who saw Lost grew up in Texas, and went to school in California. He's teaching in Corvallis and then working three days a week with a veterinarian in Eugene, where he lives. And then he volunteers one day a month out here in Florence. Taj doesn't have his own practice."

I'm pretty sure my little brother wanted to know about Lost's exam, not about Dr. Mazari's education and work. Geno is probably confused, but he's so sweet that he only nods. Mom keeps talking. "If we had to go to one of the vets here in town, it could cost us over three thousand dollars to get Lost's teeth taken care of."

I don't know where she got this amount because it's right in the paperwork that his care would be between $1,200 and $2,500! So Mom's exaggerating. I think about correcting her, but I decide there's no point. If Mom believes we're saving that much money, it means she's in an even better mood.

A few moments later, Mom laughs as she tells Geno how excited Lost was when she arrived at the humane society and how he spun around in the air and it made Taj laugh.

Dad laughed a lot.

People who laugh are happy, and that's how I remember Dad.

Mom and Geno keep talking and I close my eyes and I see Dad in his green coat and his yellow fishing hat. He's chewing sunflower seeds, which the dentist said were bad for his teeth, but Dad ate them anyway. He loved the salt.

Dad also loved sour pickles, spicy chicken tacos, and sweet potato fries.

He loved ripe peaches in the summer and fresh strawberry pie, which Mom makes with real whipping cream that goes on top.

Geno and I have a routine we do sometimes before we go to sleep where we ask Mom to tell us Dad's favorite things. The list changes, but I'm not sure Geno notices. If Mom's tired, I think she just says her own favorite things, because I'm not sure Dad liked red licorice better than chocolate, or that he liked jasmine-scented candles or watercolor pencils. But maybe he did.

I know he loved his boat, which we couldn't save after The Accident, because it sank and was a wreck when it was finally pulled out of the river. Mom said we should have gotten more money from the salvage place.

Here is what I know for certain: Dad loved crabbing.

He loved Mom.

And Geno.

And me.

10.

I FALL ASLEEP EARLY, AND WHEN I WAKE UP IT'S NOT morning.

It's late at night. Right away I notice Lost isn't next to me. I look over at Geno's bed. He's on his side and he's got his two hands tucked under his cheek. He looks so peaceful. He's wearing the top to his Maui Halloween costume. It's amazing that after everything that's happened to us, my little brother is still the most optimistic person in the whole world. He always goes to sleep believing tomorrow will be great.

I decide to go look for Lost because maybe the chopped-up rotisserie chicken gave him an upset stomach. He might be waiting by the door to go out. He's too polite to wake me.

There's light coming from the living room. I peek around the corner and see Mom lying on the couch under a blanket with Lost sleeping on her feet. The glow is from her cell phone.

Mom hasn't heard me. She's too busy looking down at her phone screen.

I realize that she's texting.

Mom doesn't text anyone at night.

Mom goes to sleep early and she doesn't ever lie down on the couch. She goes into her room and she shuts the door.

Something must be wrong, but then I see she is smiling. People don't do that about bad news. So maybe she's telling one of her friends a joke. But Mom doesn't tell jokes because she's not "a fan of punch lines." She says the things she thinks are funny just happen in life.

I watch Mom and I wonder what's going on. Half the time she's asleep before me and Geno. She works hard at the restaurant and she's on her feet for hours. Plus, since Dad died, she says she just needs to shut her eyes at the end of the day and make the world slow down.

Right now Mom looks wide-awake.

I can see the clock and it's 11:37. I open my mouth to say something, but then Mom laughs and starts texting again, so I change my mind.

I turn and go back to bed.

My sheets and my pillow are still warm.

I wonder what was so funny on Mom's phone. I could have asked her.

I have a bad thought: What if she is texting the veterinarian?

Earlier, I looked up the name Taj. It means "crown." Dr. Mazari is no prince, that's for sure.

I'm not telling Mom about his name. There is a super famous building in India called the Taj Mahal. It said online that it has become a symbol for love. Ugh. That's so gross. Buildings are buildings. They shouldn't be symbols and especially not for love. But Dr. Mazari's family is from Pakistan, not India, so maybe the building means nothing in this situation. It did look really interesting in the pictures. Maybe one day I'll go visit there.

I try to fall back to sleep, only I'm having trouble letting go of my thoughts.

Then I realize Mom could be texting *anyone* on her cell phone. Not necessarily the veterinarian.

She has her best friends, Taffy and Madeline. She is probably telling them all about Lost and his crummy teeth. And then there are the other waitresses and waiters and cooks at work. She loves them. Plus, she has friends in Coos Bay, where she went to high school. She really likes Button's parents. And Jose's too. We meet sometimes at the beach and have "windy picnics." That's what we call the Sunday afternoons when we show up with food and no matter how hard we try, half our stuff ends up getting blown away.

Mom being awake so late and texting doesn't necessarily have anything to do with a doctor named Taj Mazari who was born in Houston and has a well-clipped mustache and a leather suitcase that turns out to have a bunch of animal medicine inside.

I fall back to sleep feeling a lot better.

The next morning, I find Mom in the worst kitchen in the world making us pancakes. I can't wait until Geno finds out. He dreams about pancakes.

As soon as she sees me, she says, "Good morning, Boo. Is Bud getting up?"

I feel so happy because she's using our special names. This morning is off to a great start. Maybe I'll even see dolphins today in the river!

Before I can answer, Mom says, "I was texting Taj after you kids went to sleep and he was able to get Lost scheduled for surgery in two weeks. Can you believe it?"

I can believe it.

I know I'm supposed to be excited, but this is exactly as I suspected late last night: Something wicked this way comes. That was a book I started and never finished, because it scared me, but I read enough to understand the general idea: A new person comes to a small town and it seems like he's going to grant wishes, but instead, it's a nightmare. Or at least I think that's what happened. I returned the book to the library once I could see things were going bad for the two kids.

It feels unprofessional for a veterinarian to be this involved in a pet owner's life.

But then I remember we haven't even paid the guy, so maybe there are different rules.

I'll have to look online and see if I can find anything about that. What if I could have his license taken away? That feels sort of mean though. So far, all he's trying to do is help our sick dog.

I snap back to attention and return to this leaky boathouse that smells fishy for a good reason. I tell myself I should just be happy that we're getting Lost's rotten teeth fixed. But I know for a fact that it's possible to feel two things at once. Because right now I'm feeling grateful *and* very anxious.

Then it gets worse, which is hard to believe.

Mom explains in a really happy way that Lost needs to have a blood test to make sure his level of something is okay before he has surgery. And what's completely crazy is that Dr. Mazari, I'm not in a million years ever calling him Taj, is driving back out here to take Lost's blood himself and we can save money and don't have to get the lab work done at a vet here in town.

This is just outrageous!

Dr. Mazari lives more than an hour away if there's no

traffic. He's only supposed to be in Florence once a month. Why would he offer to do so much driving? And because of this "act of incredible generosity," Mom has invited him to have an early dinner with us. But she's not even going to cook in the worst kitchen in the world. She says we're going to Curly's Seafood and we are getting the best table, which is by the window!

My head is spinning.

That's just an expression, because of course even an owl doesn't have a head that actually spins all the way around. But that's what it feels like.

I've lost my balance in this world.

Not even pancakes can make me feel better.

Mom's still really happy when she drops us off at school. Geno's also really happy because his day started with maple syrup. I'm really unhappy, but I try to hide it.

It's hard to pay attention in class. The math teacher is talking but the words pass right through me because my thoughts today are bigger than decimals and percentages.

I have made a plan. When Dr. Mazari comes out, it's important for me and Geno to be monsters. We can do it. But the hard part is that we're going to need to be monsters in a very sneaky way. The more I think about it, the less sure I am that Geno is up for the job. He won't understand. And he'd for sure go squeal to Mom.

I guess I'll have to be a solo monster.

At lunch I tell Button what's going on and her face scrunches up.

"Cordy, I don't get it. Some guy is helping with your new dog and you're mad about that?"

"I told you the veterinarian had a mustache, right?"

"The problem is you don't like this guy's mustache?"

"No. That's just an added thing. He sort of has a beard too. Or else it's just really bad shaving."

"It's a style," she says. "He's helping your dog for free. Forget about anything else. That's my advice."

I didn't ask for advice, I just wanted Button to listen. "Everything has a price," I mumble.

I'm not sure what I even mean, but Dad used to say that sometimes. I obviously haven't explained in the right way about Dr. Mazari, because if I had, Button would understand. But she goes on to another topic before I can stop her.

"The real-life skills thing is due next week. Have you done it?"

I roll my eyes. Some parents spoke up at a school board meeting last summer and they said important stuff is being left out of what we are being taught. The idea of who decides what kids should be learning caused a lot of headaches. So at the start of the school year, they gave us a list of things we're supposed to know how to do. They call it our "Real-Life Skills Report Checklist." It's homework, but not the regular kind. Last Tuesday they handed out a worksheet we're supposed to fill out with everything we've accomplished during the year. Button takes the paper from her backpack to look.

"Okay, the first thing is: Make a meal without help."

I just shake my head. "Yeah, that's so easy. Even Geno can do it."

"Josh Berger said his idea of a perfect meal is eight microwaved chicken nuggets and a bag of chips."

"Does that qualify? It's irritating if it does," I say, though the fact is that we eat a lot of frozen Tater Tots, so making a meal without help is mostly heating up stuff Mom left for us. But I'm still alone putting together dinner a lot. In Button's house her dad does all the cooking. He doesn't follow recipes; he just tosses all kinds of things into pans. It's pretty good most of the time.

Button is staring at the list. She reads, "You need to be able to start the dishwasher and the washing machine on your own."

"They shouldn't think everyone has those things. I mean, we had a dishwasher on Buckskin Bob, but we don't in the boathouse."

"Yeah. Nina lives in a trailer. I don't think they have a dishwasher *or* a washing machine."

I've never been over to Nina Reynolds's house. She's older than us and swims with Button. I don't know if she has big feet. Sometimes I can't help but feel competitive with Button's swim team friends. Now I just feel bad thinking about Nina not having a washing machine or a dishwasher. We didn't have a washer and dryer when we first moved into the boathouse. Mom asked if it was okay for us to use the ones in the Big House, and instead, the McKerns bought us our own machines. They are the stacked kind, which Mom says are too small and that's why we have to do laundry all the time. The machines are crammed into the area that used to have shelves to hold food in the worst kitchen in the world, so we don't have any counter space now. I'm not complaining, but the dryer doesn't vent the right way. Mom says we might be eating lint that we can't see. I don't worry about it, because there's so much else to get a headache over.

Button eats more of her sandwich and then reads the next life skills assignment: "Learn how to pack a suitcase." She snorts. "Packing is no big deal!"

"When we moved to the boathouse, we just put our stuff in boxes that we got from behind the wine store. We don't have any suitcases. We've never taken trips anywhere."

"Now you have that cool backpack for when you travel."

"Yeah, except I don't travel."

"I've got my swim bag and a duffel I use for meets. Packing really isn't hard. You just take clothes out of the closet and put them in something. Cordy, there's a whole area at Goodwill with used suitcases. They don't have wheels, so no one wants them if you end up going somewhere."

"The hard part would be figuring out *which* clothes. So maybe it should have told us: 'Learn *what* to pack in a suitcase.'"

Button lowers her voice, which isn't necessary because it's loud in the lunchroom and no one is listening to us. "The last time my great-aunt Gertie came to visit us, she packed her socks in an empty Kentucky Fried Chicken bucket."

"Ewwww. Was it still greasy?"

"She said she really cleaned it first. But River kept smelling her ankles the whole time Aunt Gertie was with us."

"River is a good dog. I bet he knew."

"Totally."

Button looks sad. "Mom says the socks in the KFC bucket should have been our first sign that Aunt Gertie was getting 'foggy-headed.'"

I only met her great-aunt Gertie a few times. I didn't smell the KFC, but I do remember that she wore headbands. Not a lot of old people do that.

Button's off from Aunt Gertie and back on life skills: "Learn how to tie a necktie."

I shrug. "That's another skill that doesn't matter to us. I don't even know anyone who wears a tie. Plus, it feels like there are probably videos to teach a person."

"I think the last time my dad had on a tie was when he and Mom got married."

I don't want to contradict her, but I remember when

he wore a tie. I mumble, "Your dad wore a tie at my dad's funeral."

Button remembers. "Oh. Yeah. Right. Sorry."

I don't want her to feel bad, so I keep the conversation going. "Mr. Busby had on a tie because he got asked to sing 'Tears in Heaven,' which Mom said was a big mistake. I hope I never hear that song again, but there's no control over something like that because they play music in stores. Mom and me heard it once at Fred Meyer and we left right away."

Button looks determined. "It's a trigger! We should tell the people at Fred Meyer not to ever play it!"

I nod. But I don't think the store chooses its own playlist. Button moves on to our next life skill: "Know the basics of self-defense." She laughs. "We know how to kick people. And punch."

"Plus, Mom told me and Geno if we really have to defend ourselves it's okay to bite and scream."

"We can't practice biting people, but we could go to the beach and scream. It might build lung power."

"Which could help you with swimming!"

I can see that Button likes this idea. She always says that part of practicing so much is to build up her lungs.

She keeps reading from the worksheet: "Know the basics of CPR."

I make a face. "We learned that with the rubber dolls."

"Yeah, and they put rubbing alcohol on Rescue Annie's

and Rescue Andy's mouths. It felt like getting bee stings!"

Just saying their names causes both of us to start laughing. The mannequins that the PE teacher uses to show "cardiac compression" are kept in the school's supply closet. They smell like mildew because they are a million years old. I guess there isn't money to buy new ones. Button manages to say, while still laughing, "We all got chapped lips from that rubbing alcohol."

"But Amber Weiss didn't because she puts on lip gloss every ten seconds!"

"Amber Weiss is so into beauty tips. I should ask her about my dry hair. I guess it's the chlorine from the pool."

"Here's a beauty tip: Don't care about your hair. It looks great."

"You've got long red hair that we all love, and you have gray eyes. You don't need to try hard."

"Thanks. I think." We're laughing again.

"There are only two things left on the list: Get money from an ATM."

I'm hot under the collar again. "That's another unfair one! Mom puts most of her money in savings, so she won't be tempted to spend. She says people who have money use credit cards, and the only people who carry money are people without much."

"You can watch my mom use the ATM. She does that when she goes to garage sales."

I like tagging along with Button's mom to look for stuff

at moving sales on Saturdays. Now I have a good excuse.

Button has reached the bottom of the page. "The last life skill is to develop a relationship with the natural world."

We both react with *derision*, which is a word I like but don't get a chance to use because I don't want to sound like a show-off. "I can't believe anyone in this town wouldn't have done that!"

Button nods. "How could you live here and not go to the beach, or into the woods? Everyone's gone camping and fishing. We see so many animals and birds."

I could tell her I saw dolphins in the Siuslaw, but I don't. Instead, I say, "I love animals. And plants. Even insects. You know what, Button, I might be more interested in the natural world than in the unnatural world."

"All I did was swim in lakes and rivers, before I switched to indoor pools." Button puts away the sheet. Her work is done. She just tricked me, because we've spent our lunchtime talking and laughing. I stopped thinking about Dr. Mazari and Mom and Lost.

The reason to have a best friend is to help pull yourself together.

11.

AT THE BOATHOUSE I CUT UP AN APPLE AND PUT PEAnut butter on it for Geno's snack. Then I get a life jacket and an umbrella and head down to the river with Lost. When I sit on the dock my sweet dog climbs into my lap and tries to get inside my coat. Today he doesn't want to be out in the rain. I understand. Sometimes you barely notice as drops fall from the sky and other days it feels like more than you can take.

We wait together for a long time, but dolphins never show up. I'm back at the boathouse just before Mom gets home. She's late and I see why as soon as she opens the front door.

She got a new haircut.

Ever since we left Buckskin Bob, whenever Mom

thought her hair was too long, I was the one to cut it. I do a good job. We have sharp scissors and I just imagine a line and cut straight across.

I stare at her new haircut and right away see what she's done: She got layers.

It's not a haircut. It's a hair *style*.

Mom has long hair and it's not red like mine and it's not curly. Her hair is light brown, which can look blond if she's in the sun. I'm not going to comment on how I think she looks, because she just fired me from one of my important jobs. I used to get ten dollars to cut her hair. But Geno doesn't think about the injustice and shouts, "Mom! You look so beautiful! You're just like Cinderella."

This is a complete and total lie.

When you think of Cinderella, you imagine a character with yellow hair up in a bun held by a headband, because she's going to the ball. And if her hair is down, which is when she's cleaning house and getting yelled at by her stepsisters, it's not a layered style. I think about telling Geno that he's wrong on all levels of wrong, but since The Accident I've somehow lost my edge as a big sister. I hope it's not damaging him in the long run by going along with him at times like this. But to make it worse, Mom likes what my little brother said about Cinderella. She laughs and gives Geno a big squeeze.

I'd like a big squeeze but I'm pretending to be very busy removing my raincoat and boots and shaking off the rain. Waterdrops fling in a lot of directions. We're supposed to do this outside, but I don't get told to stop.

I can't help but think that maybe Mom got this hairstyle, which had to cost a lot more than the ten dollars she pays me, because of Dr. Mazari, who she wrongly calls Taj. Geno doesn't even know that *Taj* means "crown" and yet he still came up with Cinderella.

I say, "I'm going to go lie down. I have a headache."

Mom looks over. "Honey, are you okay?"

I'm not okay, but I shrug. "I'm just worn out."

Mom accepts my very bad explanation and goes to start dinner. I see her toss her hair, which is not something she usually does. It's so irritating.

Once I'm in my room I fling myself onto my bed. It's a big move, but no one sees, which makes it a waste of time. I try to focus. I need a real strategy for when Dr. Mazari shows up tomorrow. A word that's not used very much is *sabotage*. I decide to look it up and I see it comes from the French word *sabot*, which was the wooden shoe people used to wear a million years ago. When workers thought they weren't getting a good deal, they would use their sabots to kick things at work.

Mom's friend Madeline once gave me a pair of wooden clogs. I don't wear them, but maybe I will tomorrow. I won't kick Dr. Mazari, but just having them on will be a reminder not to let down my guard.

I need to take my mind off being a solo monster, so I

decide to look at the tide chart online, which is something I've never done before. Dad did it every day. As soon as I do, I feel more connected to him.

Dad had a tide app on his phone. I use Mom's computer. Dad said that a long time ago, before the internet had the answers, his father would take out a little booklet that people bought every year to make tide guesses. Dad kept one of them to remind him of Pop-Pop. It had a blue cover with ads for fishing stuff.

I bet it got thrown away.

Dad said the little booklet had "only sentimental value" because the tide changes every day. Dad checked the tide chart to find "slack water." That's when the tide isn't coming in or going out. It happens either at the end of high tide or the end of low tide, and it doesn't last very long. At that time the pull on the ocean calms down and a crab can move around more easily looking for stuff to eat, which is what a crab does as a round-the-clock job.

Dad liked to get all his crab pots in place an hour before slack water. They aren't actually pots, but that's what the traps are called. They're special-made cages and you wire the bait inside, which for Dad was mostly dead fish. The law in Oregon is that crabs have to be at least six and a quarter inches across the shell or you can't keep them. Dad's pots had escape rings, so the smaller crabs mostly got out themselves before the traps were pulled up. And another rule is that you can only take male crabs. Dad called the females "she-crabs." They have claws with red tips, and males don't. When I was really little, I thought it was because she-crabs were wearing nail polish.

I shut Mom's computer and think about Dad on his boat. I whisper, "I miss you."

No one is around to hear me.

In the morning I come out of my room to see Mom's hair doesn't look the same because she slept on the new style and the layers got squashed. I can't say I'm glad that Dr. Mazari isn't going to get the full effect of her paying all that money for a professional cut. But it's still pretty great. I would tell her only I still think it was a UE. And we've been taught that unnecessary expenses are not good. She's happy, so I decide not to take that away.

Mom has work, only it's a teacher in-service day, so us kids don't have to go to school. Mom drops off Geno at Jose's house. They made a plan to borrow a metal detector from Dad's old friend Ducky, and then search for stuff on Heceta Beach. In October, Geno and Jose used Ducky's metal detector and made fifty dollars. That morning they'd seen a sign in the beach parking lot asking for help finding somebody's lost car keys, so they looked for two hours and then found them. They aren't going to ever forget getting the reward. They've gone searching for stuff a lot since, but they bring home only old bottle caps.

The boys are too young to be on the beach alone for

very long, so Jose's mom always goes with them. She knits custom baby blankets to make extra money, sitting in a lawn chair under an umbrella while the boys search for treasure. I wonder if she gets sand in the yarn. It gets carried by the wind. In the boathouse it comes in from our shoes, Lost's feet, and all our clothing. Mom says when she vacuums, she wins the battle, but that she'll never win the war on sand. But when she saves up enough money and we leave this place, she will say goodbye to sand forever. It's a terrifying thought.

Once Mom and Geno are gone, I shout for Lost. I get the life jacket and we make our way down the zigzagging trail through the brambles and ferns toward the dock. There are wild lilies that bloom this time of year. Dewdrops hang on the thin pink and yellow petals. I stop and lean close. I've seen pictures of flower arrangements in magazines and these little plants are more beautiful than any of those. I used to pick them when I was younger. Now I let them be.

As soon as I get to the dock, I see a salmon trawler heading up the Siuslaw. I wave at the boat because I know it's Dad's friend Ducky. Sometimes if Ducky's had a good catch, he leaves us a cleaned salmon in a cooler filled with crushed ice. Mom grills the fish and it lasts for days. I don't mind leftovers, but there's only so many salmon salad sandwiches a person can eat.

I hope Ducky doesn't drop off a salmon today.

Mom has said I should be grateful for other people's generosity and I need to "never look a gift horse in the mouth." I had no clue what she even meant because how many people go around giving away horses? It turns out you can tell a horse's age by looking at their teeth. Young horses are worth money. An old horse not so much. I guess if someone gives you a horse, it's rude to right away stare into their mouth to see how much your present is worth. I would never do that because I don't want to get bit by a horse.

When the McKerns leave the Big House, there are always a lot of empty wine bottles in the recycling bin. I was curious, so I took three of the dark green bottles and googled the wine labels. I was shocked to see how much money the stuff cost! The McKerns gave Mom a bottle of wine as a present when they left last time, and I was thinking we could sell it to add to our savings account. But when I looked a gift wine bottle in the label, it was fifteen dollars. Mom said she wasn't drinking it and planned on giving the wine as a holiday present to Taffy. I didn't tell her that what the McKerns drink costs five times as much. I don't want her to feel bad.

After a while I leave the dock and head back up the trail to the Big House, where I slip off my life jacket and get my backpack and water bottle. I know the shortcut to the beach just north of the jetty. I decide that I'll take Lost for a walk on the beach.

I watch my funny little dog run around trying to investigate the piles of what he thinks are live crabs. The months of May and June are when female Dungeness crabs molt. They have to do this to grow. Lost's not completely wasting his time, because there can be little pieces of crab marrow still stuck in the shells. They don't all make a clean break. A crab isn't safe without a hard covering, so after they wiggle out of their shells, they hide under the sand while they grow a new skeleton, which is on the outside of their bodies. That's how to think of the shell. Doing this takes only a few days. What is it like to leave behind the thing that protects you? I wonder if crabs are afraid to grow up.

Dad said that a crab molting was like me getting a new pair of shoes. I said, "Yeah, but I don't spend three days in the sand *growing* new ones."

Lost and I lose track of time.

I look from my dog out to the ocean. After a while, I notice that Lost isn't sniffing at the crab shells anymore. He's trailing right at my heels. He's probably gone twice as far as me since he's been running frantically in all directions. I forgot that I'll have to turn around and cover the same distance to go back home. I can see that Lost is tired, so I find a big piece of driftwood and I sit down so that he can rest. Lost climbs up into my lap. When I look down, his eyes are shut and he's already asleep. He's taking medicine now and he has bad teeth. I wish I hadn't gone so far. Up ahead I can see the outline of the Driftwood Shores Resort on Heceta Beach. That's where Geno is supposed to be with Jose looking for buried treasure. I put Lost in my backpack and start walking. The little guy doesn't even wake up.

Until we found Lost, I didn't know dogs could snore.

There are only a few people out, but I see Jose's mom. She's in her folding chair knitting one of her blankets. If the wind gets any stronger, her umbrella will blow over. I've known Mrs. Lopez since Geno started kindergarten. I feel like she understands about The Accident because she doesn't bring it up all the time, asking "So how are you doing?"

People do that a lot. Only no one wants to hear a kid say "I'm not doing great." It's good not to have to lie about how I'm feeling.

Mrs. Lopez looks up from her knitting when she sees me coming. She calls out, "Cordy!" I wave and head over to take a seat on a log next to her. I can see Geno and Jose are walking near the water with the metal detector. Geno has a small shovel and a sieve. When Jose thinks they've found something, Geno digs and then dumps the sand in the plastic sifter. They shake it in a really hopeful way.

"Did you walk all the way here from home?"

I nod. Lost wakes at the sound of her voice and his head pops up from the backpack. He seems embarrassed that he's being carried like a baby and he scratches to get out. I pull down the zipper and Lost wiggles free. He takes off after Geno, which makes Mrs. Lopez laugh.

"He's a good dog."

"He's a *very* good dog," I tell her.

Mrs. Lopez nods. "I'll give you a ride home. The boys already had a twenty-minute warning."

Mrs. Lopez goes back to working on her blanket, which is nice because it means she doesn't expect me to have a conversation, even though she can knit and talk at the same time. I keep my eyes on Geno and Jose. They are pushing each other and laughing. I guess the fun part of searching for treasure is being on this huge beach with no one telling you what to do.

It's believing that anything is possible.

I'm going to try to believe that too.

12.

WE ARE WAITING FOR DR. MAZARI TO SHOW UP.

Mom is not acting like herself. She put on lip gloss, which she almost never does, and she's wearing a sweater she borrowed from Taffy that is the color of tomato soup. I feel like adults should not borrow clothing from each other. That's a kid thing to do. She's also wearing earrings that dangle. She always wears earrings that are just "posts." And she wears the same ones all the time. They are from Dad and they have little red stones, which are garnets, not rubies, only who can tell from a distance? I've seen these dangling earrings in her jewelry box, but the one time I remember her wearing them, she said they were a real pain because they hit her neck if she turned her head fast.

I guess she's not planning on moving her head very much.

I will admit that she looks really good. But she always looks really good, so I don't think the borrowed sweater or the new layered haircut or the dangling earrings should get the credit.

Now that I've seen what Mom's wearing, I go to my room and put on the one piece of clothing I saved from Dad: his old green hoodie. I take off my regular shoes and put on my wooden clogs.

When I come out, Mom says, "Cordy, you want to wear that to dinner?" She sounds confused, since I've never worn it before. I've kept the sweatshirt in the back of our closet, which is really just an area with old wooden pegs that once held fishing nets. Mom put a folding screen in front of it.

I've had to roll up the sleeves on the sweatshirt because they are way too long, and now it looks like I've got big green doughnuts around my wrists. The hood hangs heavy on my spine. Dad's old sweatshirt is so long, it goes almost to my knees. I hope no one I know sees me in this thing! But then I remember we are going to Curly's Seafood and everyone who works there is a family friend, plus there is a chance someone from school could be eating dinner there for a special occasion. Also, Dad's old green hoodie is so hot. My face feels sweaty and all I want to do is take it off. But I will be strong.

I bet Dr. Mazari shows up in a yellow convertible with

the top down. The wheels will have spokes and the steering wheel will have a leather cover. The seats inside are probably going to be red.

Dr. Mazari arrives in a gray van.

And he's right on time, which is irritating. Geno immediately grabs the side door to look inside. Mom tries to stop him, but Dr. Mazari doesn't have a problem with him opening it. I can see the van is filled with animal crates like the one Pierre from the Big House uses. There are also old blankets and a pile of leashes, collars, and pet toys.

I'm so disappointed. Geno wants to try to climb into the biggest dog crate, but Mom stops him. Dr. Mazari explains he uses his van on the weekends when he does rescue work, picking up dogs and cats that might not make it without someone stepping in. He says he keeps a big list of people who help foster and find homes for the pets in Lane County.

This guy is killing me.

Mom wants to know everything about the animal rescuing. Geno wants to know more about the van. I want to know when I can take off this hoodie. It may have mildew on it, because I keep smelling mold. Our roof has leaked over the area with the pegs. The drips didn't seem like much of a problem compared to the kitchen, but I guess we were wrong to ignore it.

When Dr. Mazari comes inside, Lost doesn't bark. This

is shocking, because Lost barks at everyone when they first get here, so there is no explanation for his behavior! Dr. Mazari stuck his fingers in Lost's mouth at the humane society and wiggled his messed-up teeth. Doesn't Lost remember? It was only last week!

Dr. Mazari has his medical satchel with him and also a brown sack with handles made of red twine. He puts down the leather luggage and then opens the bag and takes out a book about heroes and legends, which is for Geno. There are a lot of pictures in the book. Geno is excited. He reaches over and gives Dr. Mazari a hug.

That is so wrong. *I've* met the guy. So has Mom. Geno has only known him for three minutes and he's wrapping his arms around the guy's waist.

I try to stay calm.

Once Geno is finished with his inappropriate squeeze, Dr. Mazari hands me a book about Boto dolphins that live in the Amazon. It was written by someone named Sy Montgomery, who is a woman explorer. I stare at the book's cover, which has a photograph of a pinkish dolphin. It's not a bottlenose and it looks very different from the one I saw in the Siuslaw. What's disappointing is this book is nothing like the autobiography of the famous music producer Clive Davis. This is something I'm actually interested in reading.

Mom looks completely surprised and I can see by her face that these presents mean a lot to her.

"I'm . . . I don't know what to say . . ." I stumble over the words.

Mom jumps in. "You say thank you."

I mumble, "Thank you."

But I'm so mad. This guy is making it impossible to hate him.

Only I'm not giving up.

Dr. Mazari opens his medical bag and takes out a syringe. Mom lifts Lost into her arms, and before our sweet dog knows what's happening, Dr. Mazari has drawn a blood sample. I'm not going to say he's really good at it, because it might have just been a lucky break. Lost shakes it off, looking confused and maybe relieved. Dr. Mazari has a small cooler in his van and he'll put "the sample" in there. In a very cheerful way, Mom says we need to get going. It's too bad the veterinarian's not heading back right away to Eugene but at least I'm going to get a slice of peanut butter pie with ice cream after dinner, and there's no way we'd be getting that without him.

We drive to Curly's in Mom's truck and Dr. Mazari follows in his van. This means he won't be coming back to the boathouse. Good.

When we get to the restaurant Geno pushes ahead of me because he wants to sit next to Dr. Mazari. Mom gives him a squeeze and says of course he can do that. Geno is really getting on my nerves big-time. I'd give him a small kick but I'm wearing these horrible clogs and it could really hurt him.

We go to the corner table by the window, and Dr. Mazari pulls out the chair for Mom. It feels like something you'd do for an old person. She can get into a chair herself. Mom smiles as if he lifted her over a swarm of ants, the stinging kind I've read about.

I wish they'd given us a different table. We're tucked away from other people. A string of little lights runs along the frame and if you look outside, you see the Siuslaw and the bridge. It's June, and it gets dark late. The sun is still up in the sky. It reflects back into the water, making the river look purple.

It's beautiful.

I really hope Dr. Mazari doesn't notice.

We don't need to see menus because we know everything they make, but Mom insists that we all take one. I want to roll my eyes, only I don't because Mom and Geno look so happy. But before we can even order a single thing, Angie comes over to our table. She says, "I'll be your server tonight." Behind her is Marko. He sets down a platter with coconut prawns and cracked Dungeness crab. There are slices of gooey cheese and wrinkled black olives lying next to teardrop peppers, carrot and celery sticks, and those fancy pickles that are the size of my pinkie finger. There are also a whole bunch of big radishes, hollowed out with edges cut like tulips. They have been filled with dipping sauces.

But that's not all.

Marko gets a basket of bread that isn't just toasted, it has been on the grill and sprinkled with olive oil and sea salt. He sets it down next to the platter. Angie and Marko both smile big. None of this is on the menu and we didn't ask for any of it.

Angie says, "A little starter for you guys from your friends in the kitchen."

Mom doesn't say anything, but Geno shouts, "¡Dios mío!"

We all look at him and Dr. Mazari laughs. Then he says something to Geno in Spanish, and my little brother answers him. Geno keeps talking and Dr. Mazari knows what he's saying and it's like they are speaking their own secret language, because for Mom and me, they are.

We are confused, but I can see something else in Mom's eyes. She's proud. In the last two years, Geno has spent a ton of time at Jose's house. I never thought about the fact that they only speak Spanish there. I thought he was just digging holes and looking for treasure or playing games. I can't believe he's been learning something. What a sneak!

Mom asks Geno to explain and he says that at first, he and Jose watched cartoons in Spanish. After a while, he realized he was starting to understand what they were saying. Then he could answer if someone was talking to him and it all sort of clicked. He is with them almost every day for hours.

It's so depressing because he's learned a real skill and it doesn't sound like he was even trying. He says he's even had dreams in Spanish. The kid seems like an open book, but he's filled with secrets.

Maybe we all are.

This Spanish thing really bugs me, and Dr. Mazari makes it all worse by explaining that growing up he only spoke Urdu with his parents. He learned Spanish in school in Texas. So I guess Dr. Mazari isn't bilingual. He's trilingual. That just feels like showing off.

I try to set a trap. "Dr. Mazari—"

"Call me Taj."

"Dr. Mazari, don't you miss your parents in Houston?"

"I do miss my parents. Very much. But both of them passed away."

Mom looks instantly sad. I didn't see his answer coming. I work hard not to feel bad for him. He's an adult without parents. That's different than a kid without a dad. He's old. I bet he's in his late thirties. It's not like he had to deal with something like The Accident.

It's quiet and awkward and then after a few moments, he adds, "I took care of them both when they got sick. I moved up to Oregon a few years ago after they were gone. I needed a new start."

Mom nods. I feel sick because she looks like she really understands. She wants to move and start over too. It's on all of her to-do lists.

This dinner so far is a nightmare, except for the starter platter that came free from the kitchen.

We eat all the food that Angie and Marko brought over and I'm not going to lie: I'm full and we haven't even ordered. I feel like the smart thing to do would be to go home. Think of the money we'd save! But Mom says we need to pick our entrees. I explain that I really only have room left for peanut butter pie. With ice cream. This makes Dr. Mazari laugh.

I don't want to make him laugh.

I try to make a case for calling it quits, only we order anyway. I end up getting chicken and not eating a single bite, but we're taking it home. I guess Lost now has his next few meals.

Geno and Mom and Dr. Mazari eat most of their dinner and then all announce they are way too full for dessert. Mom says, "Let's just skip it."

It's the last straw.

I stand and take off Dad's old sweatshirt. I wish I could ditch the clogs, but I can't walk out of here barefoot. Tears start to run down my face. Mom gets up from her chair and tries to put her arms around me but I turn and head out the door.

I sit down on the bench right outside the front of Curly's. It's for people to wait for their names to be called when there aren't tables. Mom comes out and asks if I'm okay. I want to say I'm sorry, but I can't.

I hate the word.

After The Accident, it's all anyone ever said. They couldn't look me in the eye, but they would mumble in a low voice, "I'm sorry." I know they were trying to do the right thing, but it didn't mean anything. *You're* sorry? How do you think *I* feel?

You should say "sorry" when you step on someone's foot, not when a person has lost their dad in a freak accident when a boat hits a wedge of sand and a big wave appears that was unexpected and it causes water to flood everything and capsize.

Mom says, "Cordy, are you okay?"

I don't answer.

"Do you want a little time to yourself?"

I still don't answer, but I manage to nod.

"I'll go get the check. We'll be right out."

I try not to watch, but I can side-eye see Mom go back inside.

Before long they are all out on the sidewalk. Dr. Mazari says he'll let Mom know whether Lost's bloodwork is okay after the lab takes a look. He's speaking to Mom and to Geno, but I think he's trying to include me. "I had a really great time."

Maybe I didn't ruin dinner.

Mom nods and says, "Me too."

Geno says, "Yo también."

You don't have to speak Spanish to know what that means.

I keep my eyes on the river. It's dark now. All kinds of aquatic life are in the water. You can't see them, but they are there. I'm not sure what's wrong with me. There is a lump in my throat. It feels like a rock. Finally, I manage to whisper, "Thank you for the dolphin book." But my voice is so low, I don't think anyone heard.

When we get home, Mom doesn't say anything about my bad behavior. I wish she would raise her voice and tell me I was a jerk. But she doesn't. She's not that kind of mom. She doesn't even seem disappointed in me.

But *I'm* disappointed in me.

13.

BUTTON IS SWIMMING IN PORTLAND AND I WANT TO GET out of the house.

So in the morning I decide to go see Old Mrs. Crowley. She once said to me that "we all have to make our own design for living." I asked her to explain and she said she means the choices we make in day-to-day life. When you're a kid so many things are decided for you, it feels most of the time like you're not designing anything. I didn't get a call to go pull weeds or sort pills into a plastic container with day of the week snap tops. I'm heading to her house because I want to do something that makes me feel better about myself. I don't have anything to carry, but I take my new backpack anyway.

I ring the bell and the door opens immediately. Old Mrs. Crowley can't have seen me out the window because she's vision impaired. She's got a sixth sense about things. It's like she's been expecting me.

"Hey there, Cordy. How you doing, child of mine?"

I try to sound upbeat, which I'm not. "I'm okay. I came over to see if you needed any chores done. For *free* today. I want to offer my services in the spirit of volunteerism."

That's close to what it says in one of the brochures Geno brought home from the library. You don't have to be a veterinarian to be a helper in this town.

"Well, lucky me! Come on and take a load off. Is it raining?" She can't see well enough to know, but she adds, "Because it sure smells like rain."

There's a word I read in a book, which no one on the planet, or at least no one in Florence, ever uses. It's *petrichor*. It means the smell made when water hits dirt. A chemical is released into the air, and humans respond to it. Camels have a great nose for the scent, which is how they find water in a desert. When I was little, I got the spelling of desert right by remembering it has one *s* and *dessert* has two, because you always want more sweets, but not more sandy hot places. I told Geno that and he said, "I'd like to eat dessert in the desert with a kid named Sandy." He's got his way of making me laugh.

Old Mrs. Crowley puts her hand out to touch my new

backpack. "What you got there?" I explain that Mrs. Hunt at the library gave it to me.

"The fabric feels high quality."

"It is."

The first thing Old Mrs. Crowley does is ask me to help sort her mail. She hands me a grocery bag full of stuff. It turns out to all be "just people asking for money or trying to sell something I don't want." There is one bill, from Central Lincoln Utility, which is for her electricity. I tell her and she says in a very dull way, "Whoop-di-doo." She's being sarcastic. She's been set up by a social worker to pay bills online, so she doesn't even open the envelope and I put everything into the recycling bin.

Once we're done with that, we go into the kitchen. Old Mrs. Crowley likes hot chocolate, but she doesn't make it unless I'm with her. She has trouble spooning the chocolate powder into the cups and measuring stuff right. I do it for both of us and then heat up the milk. She only microwaves to cook now because she can't see if she's burning something, but she lets me use the stovetop. While I'm at the burner, she asks, "What's on your mind today? Something got you out of whack?"

She might not be able to see, but the woman can feel.

I shake my head like nothing's wrong, then I remember I need to use words. "My mom has a new friend."

"Okay."

"I introduced them."

"But you don't like this new friend?"

"I like him okay. I don't know him. And she doesn't know him. We just met the guy. Geno loves him, but–"

"Geno loves everyone."

"Exactly." I'm so glad she gets it. I'm not going to tell her we found out my little brother speaks Spanish. She is already on Team Geno.

"So what bothers you about your mom having a new friend?"

That's a gut punch because I can't answer. Why do I feel angry? And afraid? Is it because Mom might make bad decisions and we'd have to move? Is it because I don't have Dad anymore?

I hand Old Mrs. Crowley her cup of hot chocolate. She takes a sip and then her whole face lights up. I think she's about to tell me chocolate is a gift, but instead she says, "I'm going to quote something to you. I memorized it a long time ago. You're just a kid, but you're brighter than a box of crayons."

I'm glad she thinks I've got brains. I say, "Thanks."

"A man named Carl Jung wrote what I'm going to say."

I'm happy she's not going to go off on Clive Davis.

"The meeting of two personalities is like the contact of two chemical substances: If there is any reaction, both are transformed."

All I can think of to say is "Oh."

She keeps going, but she's not quoting anymore. "So maybe having a reaction to your mom's new friend means something important might happen to *you*. As well as your mom."

"No offense to Carl Young, but I think the important thing is only happening to Mom. She got a new hairstyle and borrowed a sweater and she was whistling this morning."

"It's pronounced *Yoong*, not *Young*, and Cordy, here's what I want you to think about: Your mom deserves to be happy."

I was about to take a sip of hot chocolate but I stop. Of course Mom deserves that! That's something I think about all the time. More than anyone on this planet, she deserves to be happy!

I can't talk about this. It was a mistake coming here, because I feel worse, not better. I have to change the subject and I have to do it fast. I blurt out, "There's another big thing going on. I saw dolphins swimming up the Siuslaw last week."

"Well, goodness! That's incredible! Anyone else see the dolphins?"

"No one but me. And Lost. And guess what. One of them was pink—which I thought meant good luck was coming my way, but I got that wrong. Being pink means the dolphin is an albino. That's very, very, very unusual. I've been going down to the river and waiting in case they come back. But they haven't. Do you think I'll ever see them again?"

"You saw them once. Isn't that enough? It sounds like an amazing thing."

I'm glad she doesn't think I made it up. I wonder if she has a point. Why do I need to see them again so badly? Maybe it's got something to do with losing Dad. Maybe what I really want is to see *him* in his boat coming up the river. I'm waiting for him to come home, even though I know that isn't going to happen. But I still can't stop myself from hoping he's going to get out of his truck and come through the door.

What if Dad hadn't gone crabbing that morning? What if Dad's boat didn't really hit the sandbar? What if we never moved and Mom was still studying to be a nurse?

That's called "magical thinking."

Maybe we don't talk enough about The Accident. At night, when the lights are out and we are in our room trying to go to sleep, Geno sometimes asks me to tell him what happened. But all I can remember from that morning is the confusion. There were people coming in and Mom couldn't stop crying. Geno was too little to understand why someone put his coat on him and took him outside to throw a ball in the rain.

There are news stories about The Accident and I guess they will stay on the internet forever. Geno doesn't know you can search for those things. When the boat capsized,

Dad was with Ricky. He usually had two people on the boat. Ricky and Piero. But sometimes Mom.

I can't think about what would have happened if Mom had been out there.

Ricky survived. He's the one who called the Coast Guard and he was the only witness. He got hypothermia from the water. That's when you're so cold, it freezes part of you. Ricky doesn't go out on boats anymore. He works for a dune buggy business that's busy in the summer but not really the rest of the year. We never see him.

After we lost Dad, people said that he was doing what he loved when he died. It was supposed to make me feel better.

But what if he had died doing something he didn't love? Would that have made it worse for us?

There is one good thing, which is I can see him in my dreams. And if I can close my eyes at night and be with someone I love, then they're still alive for part of my life.

I'm looking into my hot chocolate. Old Mrs. Crowley says it tastes better in an orange cup. I guess I believe her. She gets to her feet and goes to a closet in her narrow hallway. She opens it and I see a lot of boxes. She puts out her hand and feels around.

"Do you want any help?"

She doesn't answer but she must have found what she was looking for, because she comes back with a leather shoulder bag. It's shaped like a fat lunch box. She unzips the top and says, "This is a Polaroid camera. Do you know what that is?"

"I don't think so."

"This camera takes a picture and then prints it out a few minutes later."

Old Mrs. Crowley pushes the leather bag across the table in my direction. She almost knocks over my cup of hot chocolate. I grab it just in time.

"I want you to take this. My photography days are behind me. Bring it with you when you look for the dolphins. Maybe you can get a picture."

"Do I need to put in paper?"

"It's not like a printer, darling. It needs special film. I have some out back." Then she sighs. "I'm sure it expired years ago, but we can get a pack and give it a try."

Old Mrs. Crowley has a metal shed behind her place. It's raining, so we take two umbrellas and head to the rusty door. She must not go out here very often, because it's hard to make the lock work. Finally, I turn the key the right way and we're inside. It's cold and also damp, but it doesn't look like the roof leaks. Go figure. The shed must have good drainage. I move a few things. There are a lot of spiders, but I'm not scared of them. They come in peace. That's what aliens from outer space usually say, but if spiders could talk, I'd suggest that as their opening line too.

Old Mrs. Crowley tells me what to look for and I move

more stuff and finally see the blue metal box she's been after. I open it and find cardboard packets.

"They say 'six hundred high-speed color instant film—two-pack, twenty pictures.'"

"Bingo! I didn't throw that stuff out because it cost a lot of money."

We go back into the house with what feels like treasure. We sit back down at the little table in the kitchen and I open one of the boxes. I remove what Old Mrs. Crowley says is a "film cartridge" but looks like a plastic piece of toast. I don't have a clue how it works, but just by using her hands to feel the parts, she's able to get it into the camera. Only, after she has the film in place, she seems doubtful. "I'm guessing the chemicals have all dried up and it won't work."

"We should put in a new battery before we try."

"No, darling. The battery is in the film pack."

"Can't we plug in the camera and charge it?"

"Nope. Doesn't work that way."

That sounds crazy to me. The film has been outside in the cold, damp shed for a million years. All that hunting for nothing. But I want to be positive, so I say, "Well, you never know."

I'm just trying to have a good attitude. I'm pretty sure this has been a big waste, but I aim the camera at Old Mrs. Crowley. "Say cheese."

She smiles, lifts her hands, and gives me two thumbs-ups. I press the button and there's a whooshing sound! Old Mrs. Crowley screams with happiness. Right away something comes out of the slot in the front of the camera.

"Well, I'll be!" Old Mrs. Crowley claps her hands. I don't want to tell her there's nothing but black on the thin plastic square in my hands. She says, "Put it down on the table. It needs time to develop."

I do what she says, but ask, "How long?"

"Only a few minutes."

She's jumpy as we wait. It's contagious, because I'm all jumpy now too. The crazy thing is that her eyes only work for light and dark and she barely sees color, and yet she finds this possible photo incredibly exciting.

Three minutes later I stare at the Polaroid picture and there is Old Mrs. Crowley! Only she looks like the people in my dreams. Her edges are blurred and she's faded. I guess the film's chemicals are worn out and they can only capture some of the light. The best part is that she looks really good. She seems younger as a ghost.

"Wow! You look great!"

"It worked?!"

"Yeah. It *really* worked."

She's so happy.

And that makes me so happy. I almost forget that I was a jerk last night and that Lost needs his teeth pulled out.

I almost forget that I might never see dolphins again in the river.

I almost forget that Mom has a new friend and he might help her leave this place.

I say, "Old Mrs. Crowley, you've made me feel a lot better today!"

As soon as the words are out of my mouth, I realize what I just called her. Then I sputter, "I'm sorry."

"For what?"

"For calling you that."

She laughs. "I'm the one who came up with the name. I started telling people, 'Just call me Old Mrs. Crowley!' It was that, or Mrs. Magoo."

I start to laugh with her.

Because of my hair, I've been called Red and Ginger. Some kids at school once started chanting "Brainiac" in a mean way after I got a science prize. And a bunch of boys down at the dock gave me the nickname Crabcake because I was with my dad on his boat so much. But I didn't mind that. Anything with cake can't be bad, and crabs paid our bills.

If I gave myself a nickname, what would it be?

Maybe The Wonderer.

I do wonder about everything.

But not The Wanderer. That's a song that's on the jukebox at Curly's. It's in what Angie calls "the moldy oldies section." I bet the guy who sings the song is a nice person, but the words make him sound like a jerk. He roams around kissing and hugging girls and he doesn't even know their names. He could get in a lot of trouble for that today.

I stay at Old Mrs. Crowley's house for another hour. Before I leave, she tells me her first name is Valerie, and I can call her Val if I want. Only her close friends do that, but not many of them are around anymore. I say I'll try. But it's going to be a hard transition.

Walking home I feel different, and not just because I had hot chocolate and I'm carrying a Polaroid camera in a leather case and packets of old film that, because of some kind of miracle of a cold shed, still work.

I'm feeling better because I made Old Valerie Crowley happy. And also, I have a great picture of her.

It starts to rain again as I walk home.

The ground under my feet gives off its sweet petrichor.

14.

MOM WANTS ME TO GO WITH HER TO CORVALLIS.

She says it's okay to miss school. Geno doesn't understand why he can't come with us, but Mom says it's better if he stays here. She's arranged for him to spend the night at Jose's house because we are getting up really early to start the drive. Once Geno hears that he'll be dropped off for a sleepover on a school night, he's way too excited to care about a long day without Mom and Lost and me.

The sky is still purple after the sunset and it's light outside when Mom says we should try to go to bed, since we have a big day tomorrow. I feel like Lost is the one having the big day, but I take a shower, brush my teeth, and get under the covers. Only I can't fall asleep.

I haven't opened the book Dr. Mazari gave me about

the river dolphins of the Amazon. I had put it in the closet on the floor underneath my summer sandals. But even though I can't see it, I know it's in there.

I go from thinking about the book to my new Polaroid camera. Finally, it's too much and I get up. Lost has been sleeping with his head on my pillow. He wakes, looks at me, and then goes right back to snoring. I take my emergency flashlight and go find the book and bring it back to bed.

The South American Boto have long pointy noses. They are toothed whales, which is what all dolphins are. I'm interested in the categories that people have made to separate animals.

I do not want to love this book.

I do not want to stare at the beautiful photographs.

I do not want this to be my favorite book ever.

The next morning, I'm awake before Mom's alarm goes off at 5:45 a.m. I peek my head into her room. She puts extra pillows under the blankets next to her when she sleeps. It looks like there's a person lying at her side. I once asked Mom why and she said that it was the only way to sleep after The Accident because when she rolls over in the middle of the night, it feels like Dad is still with us.

In those early days when we went from four to three living on Buckskin Bob, everyone who came to our house brought us cookies. What they didn't know was we had no appetite. Even Geno, who loves cookies, didn't want any. The way I knew we were getting better was when we could eat chocolate chips again.

It's eighty-two miles from Florence to Corvallis. It will take us an hour and a half to get there. We have to be at the Oregon State University Veterinary Teaching Hospital at 8:00 a.m., so we need to leave the boathouse at 6:15 a.m. to have time to park "in case of the unexpected."

Our family had the unexpected.

So now we expect it.

Mom's talking out loud, not really to me, going over the steps of the day. She didn't borrow a sweater and she's not wearing dangling earrings. She has on jeans and a blue shirt that is very soft because she's had it forever. Her hair is pulled back and held with a clip. She's not wearing lip gloss, but she looks incredible.

Mom drinks her coffee and I'm allowed to have a small sip. I can't wait until the day when I can just "fuel up," as Dad used to say. I eat cereal and Mom has a toasted English muffin and a poached egg. I love the word *poached*. Some words are more fun to say than others.

Mom tells me to gather what I want to have with me for the day because Lost won't be released until late in the afternoon. I put my Polaroid camera and a box of film in my backpack. I add my favorite sweater, a notepad, some colored pencils, a hairclip, and half a pack of spearmint gum. I have a picture of Dad in a small gold frame. He never met Lost, but I know Dad would want the best for him. I decide I'll take the photo. On the end of my bed is one of Lost's plastic water bottles. I decide to bring it too.

I start to zip the bag shut, but then I stop.

I want to have the book Dr. Mazari gave me. Because what if robbers come into the house while we're gone and one of them is interested in wildlife and they take the book? I stuff it in my backpack, which is really heavy now. I start thinking about the life skills checklist. Maybe "learn how to pack" wasn't such a bad idea.

When we head out the door, Lost is confused. He doesn't understand why he didn't get his breakfast. He cries a little bit when Mom puts his leash and harness in the back seat.

Once we are driving, I turn to Mom. "Thanks for letting me come with you."

She smiles, keeping her eyes on the road. "It was Taj's idea. He thinks one day you might want to study science at a university."

I don't say anything because air is stuck in my lungs. What is wrong with this guy? Why is he thinking about *my* future?

I wish I hadn't gotten the day off from school. But it's too late. There are people in my life who know things about education. Mom was studying at the community college before The Accident. Old Valerie Crowley has an accounting degree from a place called Sacramento State. She calls it "Sack of Tomatoes State." I'm going to ask her more about it next time I see her, but not because of anything Dr. Mazari believes about me one day studying science.

I stare out the window.

I force myself to think about something else.

I like the drive going east because the first fifteen miles of Route 126 run right along the Siuslaw. Most of that time you can see the river, but it splits in places, turning into two streams with green land in the middle. There are a few houses out there and I wonder what it would be like to live surrounded by water. Little bridges cross marshy areas to get to these places. Do the people go to sleep every night worrying about flooding? Or at some point, when dangerous possibilities are all around you, maybe you forget to worry.

Did Dad do that? Did he stop seeing the ocean as a risky place?

I see dozens and dozens of finches and sparrows on the electrical lines. Lost would love running out onto the green islands looking for rabbits and squirrels and chasing after the birds. But he's on my lap, half asleep. He doesn't take long car rides. He's a stay-at-home dog.

I keep one hand on his back to let him know he's not alone.

We get to Corvallis early, which is how Mom likes to do things. We find the building where Lost will have his teeth pulled and we get a good parking space very close by. Lost looks happy, walking with a bounce in his step as we go inside. He doesn't know what's about to happen. The paperwork has been filled out online in advance and Mom only has to sign a release. I feel like I might cry when the man behind the counter comes out and takes Lost. Our little dog suddenly looks so afraid. He starts to shake. It's more than I can handle. I want to give the man Lost's water bottle, but I can't do it. I don't want the guy to think we can't afford a real dog toy.

We are getting ready to leave when Dr. Mazari comes in. He apologizes for not being there when we arrived. Mom says we were early and we didn't think we'd see him.

Dr. Mazari says it's going to go great and we shouldn't worry.

Mom says we aren't worried, which is a lie.

Dr. Mazari says the procedure will take a while. He'll call us when it's over and maybe we can have lunch.

I say, "I'm not hungry."

Mom manages a smile. "Maybe you will be in four hours when it's lunchtime."

She's right, but I can't stop myself from being "difficult."

It's early and everyone is just waking up as we walk around the campus. The first thing I notice is that so many of the buildings are made of bricks. They're really big and look very important. One place has columns, which I've never seen before in real life. The structure has a dome for a roof. Whatever this kind of architecture is, I think banks try to copy it. Mom downloads something on her phone that tells where we are and what we're seeing. As we walk, she points out lecture halls and dorms, which are where students live. They have more than one library here, and everything is surrounded by trees and lots of open grassy areas. It's like we are in a huge park that has streets and paths. College students walk or ride bikes. Mom says that more than 46,000 people go to school here. I almost fall over. I ask, "And Dr. Mazari is a teacher?"

"He's an adjunct professor."

"What does that mean?"

Mom knows I'm interested in words. She takes her phone and types *adjunct*. She reads to me, "*Adjunct*. A thing added to something else as supplementary rather than an essential part."

"So he's not essential?"

"I think it means he's part-time."

"Then why don't they just call him a part-time professor? I guess in college they like words to sound fancy and important." I don't mean to sound bratty, but it comes out that way.

Mom doesn't answer. Maybe she thinks it sounds fancy too.

We keep walking and she says, "He's had a lot of education."

I know the "he" is Dr. Mazari.

I repeat something Dad once told me about himself. "Dad went to the School of Hard Knocks. He said it was the University of Life."

Mom doesn't respond.

She went to that school too.

We keep walking. We cross a big sports field and then check out an auditorium, but only on the outside. Mom asks if I want her to carry my backpack and I say no. It's heavy and she might realize I have the dolphin book inside. I say, "I like carrying my new backpack. I've seen a few of the college students with the same one."

That's true and it made me feel good. I'm not sure why.

As we keep looking at the university, I can see Mom thinking in a serious way. We walk by the Linus Pauling Science Center. I know that the character Linus is in the very old comic called *Peanuts*. He was the one who had a blanket. I don't think his last name was Pauling.

Suddenly it starts to rain, so we move under an awning. We stand in silence and then Mom says, "Your dad could have gone here and studied anything he wanted. He was very smart. He didn't have the kind of opportunities you and Geno will have."

I want to ask her how she knows what kind of opportunities Geno and I will have, but I don't. Does she feel bad that Dad graduated from high school and then went straight into Pop-Pop's crab business? Dad loved the boat and he loved the ocean. We can feel bad forever about The Accident, but not about his job.

Only I don't say that.

We watch the gray sky and I can see that Mom is getting jumpy. She puts up the hood on her coat and takes my hand. "I don't mind walking in the rain."

We haven't held hands in a long time. I try to remember when and decide it might have been at Dad's memorial. I sometimes take Geno's hand if we are going to cross a street. I'm too old to be doing that if people are watching. But I like holding Mom's hand. Her fingers are warm and she's giving me a little squeeze. It makes me feel like she's not just at my side, she's *on* my side.

We keep walking at our own pace.

We don't care if the world sees us.

The rain hits our faces and no one can tell the difference between the raindrops and our tears.

15.

DR. MAZARI CALLS MOM'S CELL PHONE AND SAYS LOST did great.

He had his teeth cleaned of tartar and plaque and he had *seven* rotten teeth pulled. I guess once they got in there, they found two more bad ones. Now his gums just need time to heal. I'm so relieved. Mom is too.

Dr. Mazari asks Mom if we want to join him for an early lunch. I can hear his voice coming out of the phone. He says, "Your sweet dog is sleeping off the anesthesia, and is in observation."

I'm not telling Mom that when we meet for lunch, he'll be in observation too.

We are going to a place on the campus called McNary. It's one of the student dining halls.

I'm glad because we've been on our feet for a long time, and who cares what I said earlier, I'm starving. We don't have to ask directions because Mom has the whole campus on her phone and she's already an expert. I look at the students as we walk. I wonder what will happen in their lives and where they will go from here.

Dr. Mazari is waiting for us out in front of McNary. Mom and I aren't holding hands anymore. She starts going faster when she sees him in the distance. I can keep up, but I don't think we need to be speed walking. It's not a good look.

The three of us go inside, and I've never been in a restaurant like this. It's really big and has so many different food options. I wish Button could see it. And also, Geno. He loves food and I know he would pile up his plate high. I spot an amazing thing in one corner: They have a machine that makes Blizzards. I'm not going to tell Geno. He would be too hurt.

Dr. Mazari says you have to be a student or work on campus or be a guest of one of those people to eat in the dining hall. We are his guests.

There aren't any other kids my age. Everyone I see must be in college and they are talking and laughing while at the same time getting food on trays. It's like they're having a party. Mom must be thinking the same thing, because she says, "I feel the young people energy." Dr. Mazari laughs. I don't think it was a joke, but then Mom laughs too. They amuse each other, I guess.

We all get different things.

I decided that I wasn't going to take anything that Dr. Mazari picked out, which is too bad because he has a slice of pizza that looks really good. After he pays for all of our food, we find a table and Dr. Mazari does his best to include me when he's talking. We have to eat fast because he teaches a class on Mondays and he needs to get across campus. I use good manners, and I listen and try to look interested. But I'm still being, as Old Valerie Crowley would say, a pill.

I like watching the other tables with the students. Mom and Dr. Mazari talk so easily. It's like Ping-Pong. I make a decision to interrupt the match. "So Dr. Mazari, you live in Eugene, but you drive here to Corvallis one day a week. And once a month to Florence. Does that mean you are a *wanderer*?"

He won't know that I'm hoping this clicks in with Mom because of the song in the jukebox. Only she might not make the connection.

He answers, "When you're a veterinarian, it's hard to get your own practice started. Until that happens, I work with animals in more than one community. And I like being able to teach. But also, to have the freedom to do volunteer work."

This was not the answer I was hoping for. Mom nods like she really understands, only she doesn't have freedom in her work. Also, she has two kids and she lives in a leaky boathouse.

I don't ask him any more questions.

Once we're finished eating, Mom says she'll walk Taj out, which is funny because we aren't in a house and this isn't her place. She tells me she'll be right back. They disappear into the crowd of loud college students and I open my backpack to get my Polaroid camera. This room feels like something I will want to remember. It would help to have a picture. Only when I take out the camera, I feel self-conscious. I think the best angle would be if I stood up on the table so I could see over everyone, but I'm not going to do that. Maybe there are pictures of this place online.

I sling my backpack over my shoulder and carry the camera. I head off in the direction Mom went, which is the main entrance. When I'm close to the doors, I look through the glass. Mom and Dr. Mazari are outside on the steps talking. It stopped raining while we were eating and the sun has poked through the clouds. The light is bright in spots. I lift my Polaroid camera and take a picture. I hold the photo and wait as the image of Mom and Dr. Mazari starts to appear. They are fuzzy on the edges and the old chemicals make it look like they are glowing in a magical way.

They aren't touching, but in the picture, they feel very connected.

Mom is tired, so we go sit in the car to wait. We put down the windows halfway and both fall asleep. When I wake up, I don't know where I am. Mom says, "I bet you'll always remember this day."

I answer, "And so will Lost."

It's after five o'clock when we are allowed to pick him up. Mom lets me carry him to the car. As we drive back over the coastal range to the ocean, Lost is on my lap asleep in a deep way. I'm silent. Mom asks, "What're you thinking about?"

I tell her the truth. "I had a dad."

"You did."

"You had a husband."

"I did."

I turn to her. She looks very sad.

I want her to be happy.

I really do.

We don't say anything for a long time. When we reach the little town of Mapleton, we go over the bridge and the Siuslaw is next to us. I'm glad I can watch the water. It is a deep green because it's picking up the color of the trees, not the sky. In the last fifteen miles of the trip home, Mom asks me if I want to sing. She knows I don't do that anymore. But here in the truck with the outside world closed off, it might be okay.

She says, "I'll sing with you. I don't have a great voice like your dad."

I tell her, "I like the way you sound." I mean that.

Mom and Dad both loved a band their parents listened to from a long time ago called The Beatles. They had a song that Dad and I always played on the boat called "Two of Us."

I say, "We could sing the song about driving nowhere."

Mom knows what I'm talking about and she laughs. She rolls down the windows and the wind rushes in. It makes it easier to sing. We start off quiet but then get really loud. Mom can't harmonize like Dad and sometimes she gets out of tune, but it doesn't matter because she tries.

The trying is the most important part.

We pick up Geno at Jose's house. He's happy to see us, but I guess he had an amazing time with his "second family." That's what he calls them now. I bet Geno will go through life being in a lot of families. Everyone wants someone who brings kindness.

When we're home, Lost is so tired that I lift him out of the car, holding him in my arms like the very first time he found me. I put him carefully on the ground, which is covered in pine needles. After he does his business, not even bothering to sniff around and find a special spot, I pick him back up. I whisper in his ear that he's going to be all right. He looks up at me with woozy eyes. I think he might be telling me that we're all going to be all right.

I take a shower and brush my teeth and I'm ready for bed. Mom is on the couch under what we call the dog blanket because Lost thinks it's his. She's texting. I don't even have to guess to who.

Geno is already asleep when I go into our bedroom. Even though it was a school night, I bet he stayed up really late at Jose's. Or maybe it was just all the excitement of having tacos al pastor for dinner.

I open my backpack and pull out my Polaroid camera, my favorite sweater, the notepad, and the colored pencils. The hairclip and the half pack of gum have fallen underneath the dolphin book. The last two things I remove are the picture of Dad in the little frame and the Polaroid I shot today of Mom and Dr. Mazari looking golden.

I put Dad back on the window ledge where I can see him best.

I take the picture of Mom and Dr. Mazari and I slip it into the book written by Clive Davis. I've never made a connection to that guy.

16.

LOST CAN ONLY EAT SOFT FOOD FOR THREE WEEKS while his mouth heals.

So he's staying on the same diet as Pierre from the Big House. Geno says we need to get him a little sweater. But for the first two days our sweet dog who has always loved to eat doesn't seem interested in his special meals. He takes a few bites but never finishes what's in his bowl.

He sleeps curled up on my bed and just wants to be left alone. He's not even excited to see a plastic water bottle. Maybe he blames us for how he feels.

Then on the third day after his surgery, while I'm getting ready to go to school, Lost climbs off the quilt and goes to the couch. I think it's a good sign. It doesn't take long before he spots a squirrel out the window. He barks like he's just seen an armed robber. The old Lost is back!

In the afternoon, he's waiting for me right at the door when I get home from school, and he looks even more like his old self. We get my life jacket and go down to the dock and sit to watch the world. There aren't any dolphins, but there are dozens of starfish on the sides of the dark rocks just below the waterline. Their real name is sea stars, but no one calls them that. Most of the ones I see are orange, but a few are bright purple. A starfish has a tiny eye on the tip of each of their five arms. I think a lot of people don't know those eyes are there. You have to be right up close to see the little spot, which is sometimes red, but can be black.

I'm glad my eyes aren't on the ends of my hands and feet.

After school I decide to go visit Valerie. I've been saying her name over and over in my mind because I have to fight calling her Old Valerie Crowley.

When I get to her place, she's sitting out front.

"Cordy?"

"It's me."

"How's the Polaroid working out?"

"Good. I don't take very many pictures because I don't want to waste the film. I put the packages in our refrigerator."

"Smart thinking. Have you seen that pink dolphin again?"

"No. I haven't seen any dolphins."

She takes some time to think and then tells me, "You don't need a picture. You know she's out there. You saw her."

"Yeah."

"I can't see much of anything nowadays. But I got it all up here." She points to her head.

I say, "You never know. The dolphins might come back."

"Embrace your life, Cordy. Don't make it about waiting."

"I won't do that." I'm not sure exactly what she's getting at, so I ask, "What do you think I should make my life about?"

"Honey, you're so smart and curious about the world. You're always learning new things. That's what I'm saying. You aren't afraid."

She's wrong, because I am afraid. But she told me once that fear eats the soul, and I don't want that to happen. I'll keep trying to find answers to all my questions. Only maybe it's okay not to solve some stuff. Maybe that's what she means.

She says, "You might want to join the singing club at school."

"You mean the choir?"

"If that's what they're calling it."

"Yeah, that's what it's called."

"And if they put on shows for the holidays, I want to go."

"I'll let you know."

I think she might bring up the famous record producer Clive Davis, but she doesn't. It's a relief.

I'm not prepared for the big news.

Me and Button are getting close to the dock. School only got out three days ago and we are free for the summer. We decided to start this morning by walking to Old Town. She's been quiet, but once we sit on a bench next to the river, she says, "Cordy, I don't want you to be mad at me."

"I won't be mad. What did you do?"

"I haven't done it yet. And also, it's not me, it's my parents. They call the shots."

I get a bad feeling in my stomach because Button's not looking at me. She's staring at the Siuslaw, which is deep green. It's low tide and we can see the muddy shore.

"Just tell me."

She doesn't say anything. That's how I know it's really bad. Finally, she whispers: "We're moving."

I'm not sure I heard her right. But then I tell myself that maybe she means moving to a new house or even to Mapleton. That's just fifteen miles away. Mapleton High School has a sailor as a mascot. But her voice sounded like something worse. So maybe she's going to Eugene. Or even Corvallis. I manage to say "Wow."

"Yeah. Wow."

"Where are you going?"

"Far."

"How far?"

"To California."

"*California*?! Why?"

"A lot of reasons. It's not one thing."

I feel like saying that it's not one thing means it *is* one thing. I manage: "Your family doesn't want to be rainy-day people anymore?"

She only shrugs.

Button has been my best friend since before kindergarten. We did our first dance class together when we were only four years old. It doesn't matter that we both quit two months later.

We've been together in this town through every school year and every holiday. We learned to swim and listen for owls at night and collect shells and fly kites and catch salamanders. We've gone camping and bowling and taken dune buggy rides. We've shared our favorite books and TV shows and movies. We learned how to make caramel popcorn and Rice Krispie Treats and decorate cakes in a class we took at the rec center. We ate lunch at the same table every day at school. We've compared homework and borrowed each other's clothes, except not shoes, because she has big feet. We've liked the same boy and gotten through it, which was easier when he didn't end up liking either of us. We both have other friends, but we've always had each other as a best friend and that's supposed to be forever.

Button was there when Dad died. She understands.

This can't be happening because it's not fair. She can't leave.

"How long have you known?" I ask.

"A while."

"A long while?"

"I was waiting for the right time to tell you."

"There is no right time to tell me."

"I know. I'm sorry, Cordy." She starts to cry. I can't stand to see her tears. I keep mine inside. I say, "It's okay. You'll be okay. We'll both be okay."

But I'm lying. I don't know if I will be okay without a best friend. I say, "In six years we'll be going to college. We can decide right now to go to the same place."

Button nods. "Yeah. We can do that."

I see her thinking in a deep way and she adds, "It might have to be a university with a good swim team. My parents hope I get a scholarship."

I don't know how much college costs, and until I went to Corvallis, I didn't picture myself even going to a university. I tell her, "They have a machine at Oregon State that makes Blizzards like at Dairy Queen. It's in the dining hall and you can get one every day if you want."

Button manages a crooked half-smile. I tell her, "When we're old enough to get phones, we can text each other every day. And we can visit on vacations."

"And we can write letters. And send things in the mail."

"Yeah. Maybe we'll be studying the same stuff, but at different schools and we can take turns doing the homework." We are trying to find a way out. I ask, "When are you moving?"

"In two weeks."

I can't believe something this big is happening so fast. It just makes no sense. But I nod like we'll stay just as close and when it's time for college we will 100 percent be at the same school with a good swim team. We will live in a dorm and be roommates.

But I don't see how that could really happen.

You have to appreciate what you have, because everything is always changing.

I keep being forced to learn the same lesson.

On Saturday, Button's going-away party is at Curly's, and Button's whole swim team is there, but of course I'm the one she sits next to.

Mom is our server and she brings all kinds of extra things that no one even ordered. When it's over, I have her take a Polaroid of Button and me outside. The bridge over the Siuslaw is in the background and the wind is blowing hard, but it's not raining. The colors in the picture come out faded because the chemicals are going bad.

It already looks like it was taken a long time ago.

We are already an old memory.

Button leaves me some of the stuff her parents said isn't worth hauling to California. We don't really have room in the boathouse, but I take the boxes because I'm not looking a gift horse in the mouth. I don't open them right away, but when I do, I find her favorite swim medal on top wrapped in tissue paper. It's gold and hangs on a blue ribbon. It says first place. Button taped a card over the part that said the name of the swim meet and she wrote "Best Friend Ever." I put it on the ledge with the picture of Dad and three of my most important Polaroids, which are Old Valerie Crowley, Lost on the dock, and Button and me in front of the Siuslaw.

Button's parents picked the town of La Cañada, California, because they have some of the best junior swim programs in the country. It turns out, saying Button will one day go to the Olympics isn't just something we used to joke about. I guess if you repeat a goal enough, and then take the right steps, it might become real. I didn't realize she was a top fifty swimmer in her age group in the country until she showed me a list with times. Number twenty-seven was Madison Hennigan. It took me a moment to realize that was her. She looked embarrassed when she told me, "I'm going to go by *Madison* in California. My Mom and Dad said I should give it a try. But you don't have to ever call me that."

I was shocked. I blurted out, "Well, I'm not going to *ever* be Cordelia!"

She said, "Cordy is a really great name."

I managed, "So is Button."

The Hennigans are leaving for California. They are pulling a U-Haul. I decide there is nothing sadder than a gray SUV with a U-Haul attached, pulling out of a driveway in a downpour. I have my Polaroid and I take a picture. Because the film is giving out, somehow the rain falling turns into thin lines that slice up the world.

I think it's the best photo I've ever taken.

Button promised to call my mom's phone when they get to California so I won't worry that they crashed.

Right before my best friend left, she said she knew I had a big life ahead of me.

I'm not sure what she meant, because the world feels smaller without her in it.

But I'm going to try to believe her.

17.

DR. MAZARI HAS BEEN DRIVING OUT TO CHECK ON Lost's mouth.

It takes about ten seconds for him to look at our dog's gums and say, "He's healing great."

I don't think Dr. Mazari spends an hour in his van just for those three words. We could make videos and send them to him.

After he's done one of his "wellness exams," he and Mom sit outside under the awning of the Big House. Or sometimes they take a walk. Geno has gone with them a few times. I'd rather stay home.

Mom is on the phone with him every night. They stopped talking about our dog a long time ago. They've moved on to new topics. I hear Mom laughing a lot. Dr. Mazari has never seemed funny to me, but I can't hear his side of the conversation.

This Saturday Mom says he's coming out for the afternoon and we're going to all do something fun together. During Covid the bowling alley closed and it's never reopened. But that might have been fun. I guess we could go see a movie. Mom says a good idea would be to drive up to Heceta Head, which is a state park. She loves the Heceta lighthouse.

Mom usually works the Saturday lunch shift, but she has taken the day off. She goes to the refrigerator and I see she has already made four sandwiches. They aren't peanut butter and jelly. They are turkey with some kind of cheese. When did she get the stuff to make those? They are on fancy bread.

Mom has our small cooler on the counter next to a pot that's permanently there to catch drops from our leaky roof, and when she lifts the top, there is ice inside and our refillable water bottles are already packed.

I didn't notice any of this earlier.

Clearly a plan was already in place.

Maybe I'm the last to know.

I'm sure we'll be taking two cars, but once we're outside Dr. Mazari says, "We can all go in my van." Before

I'm able to ask how we'll do that with all the animal crates and no place to sit, he slides open the door. There is a back seat that wasn't there before. Geno is excited and climbs right in. Lost jumps in after my little brother, but I take my time. When I sit down and put on my seat belt, I realize the strap is brand-new.

I really hope none of these changes have anything to do with Geno and me! Dr. Mazari would be making a lot of wrong assumptions about his future.

I need to think fast. After he starts the engine, I say, "This van feels like the kind of place where I could get motion sickness. I hope I don't throw up."

Mom turns around. She's smiling but in an awkward way. "You'll be all right, honey. It's only a short drive."

She knows it's more than twenty minutes to the lighthouse. That's not short.

I have Lost in my lap and as we start down the driveway, I actually hope I'll vomit. That's happened to me only one other time while in a car, but if I shut my eyes, I might be able to get nauseous. Especially if I sway from side to side.

Unfortunately, even with my eyes closed and my rocking motion, I'm fine when we turn off Highway 101 and circle down under the Cape Creek Bridge to enter the state park. There are just two other cars in the lot and I see only a handful of people. I wish I'd brought my Polaroid camera. I'd take a picture of the lighthouse, which

I think is one of the most photographed things on the Oregon coast. In school we learned it was on the National Registry of Historic Places.

Heceta Head is pretty great. There is a sandy beach, and the rocky shoreline on both sides makes the cove amazing. Cape Creek is wide and runs down from the Coastal Range and it goes straight across the beach and into the ocean. High up on a cliff on the north side is the famous old lighthouse and next to it is where the lighthouse keeper once lived. There are two really big rocky islands just beneath the lighthouse and lots of tidepools on the cove edges.

Once we are out of the van, Dr. Mazari explains to Geno the difference between seals and sea lions. I force myself to only half listen, which is hard because I am interested in what he's saying. I'm not sure Geno is.

Geno wants to dig holes and make tunnels. Dr. Mazari drops to the sand with him, saying, "Let's get to work."

Lost has his nose low and is excited to explore a new area. There's only one other dog down here, but Lost has no interest in meeting a dachshund who's wearing a swimming vest and he takes off in the other direction. I like that attitude.

I slip out of my shoes and go near the water's edge, being careful not to make contact with any of the waves. I wade across the creek, which isn't very deep. It doesn't scare me because it's freshwater, not the wild, salty ocean.

No one is on this side of the beach and being here makes me feels more independent. I walk carefully on the hard-packed sand, never going closer than a few feet from the water. I'm looking for interesting shells and I stop worrying about Dr. Mazari. I glance back a few times at Mom sitting on the dry sand. She has the cooler at her side and the wind makes her hair dance into the air.

I lose track of time.

My ears and nose feel cold when I look up to hear Lost barking.

It's not random yapping; it's what he does when he's excited. I see him standing on the rocks at a distance on the left side of the cove. He's far away from Mom and Geno and Dr. Mazari, so they can't hear him over the crashing waves.

I wait for him to stop, but he doesn't.

I shout, "LOST!"

There's a man close by and he turns to see what's wrong with me. I wave him off, calling out, "It's the name of my dog, I'm okay." The guy looks confused but goes back to his beach walk. Shouting for my dog isn't going to work anyway, so I decide I better go check out the problem.

I leave the beach and go to the sharp rocks to find Lost, who's still barking and staring down into a tidepool.

I take a few steps closer to see purplish sea urchins. They have spines that wave up at me. There is a big piece of brown kelp, and two orange starfish. I don't know why my dog finds this so upsetting.

But then at the bottom of the tidepool, I spot a clear plastic water bottle.

Lost's favorite thing!

"Really, Lost? A plastic bottle?"

Lost's tail is swinging wildly back and forth. It's like he's saying, "YES! A plastic bottle!"

Then I take another look. Is there something inside the bottle? The light makes it seem as if it's filled with gray liquid. I bend down as close to the water as I can. I'm so worried that I might fall in. There could be a sneaker wave.

I start to back away, when suddenly I see motion in the plastic bottle.

I watch as the container, which is trapped between two rocks, moves a few inches.

Then I realize there's an octopus in the bottle!

It must be trapped.

I gasp.

I have to go for help.

I stand up. I'm on the rocks, barefoot.

Every step is tricky.

But when I reach the sand, I take off in a run. With Lost at my heels, I sprint across the wide creek and water splashes up in all directions. I arrive half soaked to a dry section of the beach where Geno, Mom, and Dr. Mazari are sitting eating sandwiches. Mom takes one look at me and says, "Cordy, what's wrong?"

I'm out of breath, but I manage: "There's an octopus trapped in a plastic bottle in a tidepool!"

I point to the left side of the cove and when I turn back, Dr. Mazari is already on his feet.

"Let's go. Show me."

I run and Dr. Mazari follows.

The plastic bottle is wedged between two rocks at the bottom of the tidepool. The waves are coming closer. I wonder how long the bottle has been trapped there.

I see the look on Dr. Mazari's face. He's as upset as I am. He's wearing running shoes, a sweater, and long pants, but he goes to the edge and lowers himself straight down into the tidepool. I look from him up at the ocean.

I'm suddenly so scared.

I don't think it's safe being in the tidepool and it's deeper than I thought. The water goes up past his waist and the rocks look sharp. He's surrounded by the purple sea urchins and I wonder if their spines are poisonous.

Dr. Mazari plunges his arm into the water but the bottle is down too deep. He tries to kick it up with his feet, but that doesn't work.

I watch as he bends down and his head goes below the surface.

I look back toward the beach. I see that Mom and

Geno are on their way. Mom looks upset. I realize she can't see Dr. Mazari. He has disappeared completely into the tidepool.

Lost is barking like crazy.

I'm really afraid.

I can't move.

Then a big wave comes in and it crashes on the rocks.

It's as if the world has gone into slow motion.

Everything is covered in a foam of bubbles. The water hits me just below my knees and I scream.

Then Dr. Mazari's head breaks the surface of the tidepool. He shouts, "Got it!" and hands me the plastic bottle.

I step back, gripping the bottle with both hands as Dr. Mazari starts to climb out of the tidepool.

But it was a lot easier getting in than getting out. All of his clothing is wet and as he tries to grip the rocks, I see blood on his fingers.

I want to help him.

I don't know how.

I look up to see another wave is coming. It's even bigger than the last one.

I shut my eyes.

When I open them, Mom is there. Geno is right behind her. She kneels down on the edge of the tidepool. Mom is strong. Is it from carrying the trays at Curly's? Is it because she does so many things every day at the boathouse? She puts out her arm and Dr. Mazari takes it. Mom pulls and it's just enough because Dr. Mazari is able to get his left foot up out of the water.

And suddenly he's standing right beside us. I lose it, saying, "I'm sorry. I'm so sorry."

But Dr. Mazari doesn't look upset. He puts his arm on my shoulder. "It's okay, Cordy. We're okay."

Mom says, "Let's get out of here."

We cross the creek and we are standing together on the hard sand.

I look down at the bottle and I see the trapped gray-green creature.

The octopus takes up the whole bottle. How did it get inside? There is no room in there.

Arms with suckers look like they are coming out of its head, which I guess is also its body. There are two eyes on top, and they are shaped like squares with black lines in the middle.

Geno bends down to see. He can't believe it. He says, "The poor octopus! Cordy, how did it get in there?"

"And how are we going to get it out?" I ask as Dr. Mazari reaches into his pocket. I see his keychain. There's a Swiss Army knife attached. He opens the blade and I hand him the plastic bottle.

We are standing close and I watch the octopus shrink back, pulling its arms together tight against the plastic. It must be so afraid.

Dr. Mazari carefully punctures the side of the bottle with the small knife. He slides the blade straight up in a perfect way and like a zipper the side of the bottle comes apart.

Dr. Mazari steps into the icy water and I'm not thinking and I go with him. He places the bottle down into the next wave.

In an instant the octopus shoots out, moving freely into the ocean. We all watch as a cloud of dark fluid appears right behind it.

"That's its defense. Octopus ink," says Dr. Mazari.

The octopus surges forward again, looking much bigger now, as it moves farther into the open sea. I see its tentacles flare wide and then close back in.

I try to keep it in sight, but the crashing waves make the water foamy, and when it clears, the octopus is gone.

Everything just happened so fast that it takes me a moment to realize I'm holding my breath.

I exhale as Dr. Mazari turns to me. "Cordy–you saved that octopus."

He's giving me the credit, but he was the one who did the saving and he has cuts on his hands and he's soaking wet to prove it. What just happened was dangerous and my whole body feels like it's on high alert. Mom puts her arm around me and pulls me in close. "Are you okay?"

I nod. I look up from the hug and realize we are all in cold water. The waves surround us.

I'm doing something I haven't done since The Accident. I'm standing in the Pacific Ocean.

Geno asks if he can have the water bottle. I think he's going to keep it, but he runs as quickly as he can across the beach to throw it away in one of the trash cans by the bathrooms.

Lost watches and looks disappointed.

In the van driving back home, we are all sitting on towels Mom brought. Lost is also wet. We did our best to clean him off, but he's gotten sand everywhere. Mom asks Dr. Mazari if it's okay if we put on the heat. Fog has rolled in, surrounding the highway and adding a heavy chill to the air.

I can't wait to tell Button about saving the octopus. She won't believe the story, or that I went into the ocean.

At first, I think the sound I'm hearing is heat coming out of the heating vents, but then I realize Geno is crying.

I whisper, "What's wrong?"

"How long was the octopus trapped in the bottle?"

"I don't know. But maybe not that long."

"I'm worried about other octopuses. What if they get in trouble because of trash?"

Mom turns around. We're whispering, but she has heard us.

"Honey, it all worked out. I don't want you to be worried."

"But–" He can't keep talking. He's really crying now.

Up front, Mom whispers to Dr. Mazari. "He's just tired. He didn't eat much of his sandwich and–"

Geno's voice is no longer a whisper. "I'm not tired. I'm mad. It's not fair that there's stuff in the ocean like that and–"

I reach over and take his hand. "It's okay, Geno–it's okay."

I look up into the rearview mirror and my eyes meet Dr. Mazari's.

I realize the last thing I'd want to do now is throw up on his new back seat.

I feel bad for Geno, but I also feel happy because we saved an octopus.

Lost climbs up into Geno's lap. It helps. Geno puts his arms around our dog and holds him close.

It's easier to do this now that Lost doesn't have such stinko breath. Geno starts to pet his wet fur and he stops crying.

I decide it's all just one more example of how sweet Geno is.

When we get home, Mom brings out a pair of Dad's old workpants that I didn't know she'd kept and one of his old plaid flannel shirts. I go get Dad's green sweatshirt. Dr. Mazari changes in the bathroom and Mom puts his clothes in the dryer, but he says he needs to head back to Eugene. I can see that Mom thought he'd wait until his things were ready. She looks disappointed, but before he leaves, he says, "I'll be out again soon. And when I do, I'll return these clothes."

Geno is standing by the door and he gives Dr. Mazari a hug.

I stay at a distance, but I mean it when I say, "Thanks for everything you've been doing for Lost, and for going with us to Heceta Head today."

He says he had a great time.

I hope that's the truth.

Mom goes outside with him and I move to watch from the front window. The glass is old and wavy and it makes everything blurry. Dr. Mazari gets in the van and Mom stays next to the door talking to him. The fog is so thick and you can't even see the Big House. It's just the van and two people in gray shadows.

Then Mom finally steps back and the van drives away.

Dr. Mazari is gone.

And for the first time I don't want him to go.

Later that night I go to the room I share with Geno. He's already asleep. I take the Clive Davis book off the shelf. I open it to where I put the Polaroid from the day at the university. Mom and Dr. Mazari are standing outside the eating place on the steps in the golden light.

I head into Mom's room and I turn on the little lamp next to her bed. It's made of blue glass and has a green shade. She got it at a garage sale and I don't think I've ever told her that it's my favorite thing in the boathouse.

I lean the Polaroid picture up against the light.

And then I go to bed.

18.

WE LIVE IN THE BIG HOUSE NOW.

It's always windy here and it turns out that the McKerns don't like the wind, and also, they hate rain. Their kids went off to college and said there's nothing to do in Florence, Oregon. They refused to spend time with their parents even in August, even when it's not so windy or rainy. So the property wasn't a good investment, at least that's what they told Taffy, who knew they were selling before anyone else and helped figure out how Mom and Taj could buy the place.

There's an upstairs and a downstairs and even a basement and a garage that can hold three cars, even though there's just our truck and Taj's van. The Big House also means that we don't have to sleep in sweatpants and thick socks when we go to bed in the winter or have a washer and dryer with a bad vent right next to the refrigerator in the worst kitchen in the world. The whole place is heated with a furnace, not electric heaters that made a beeping sound that always startled Geno.

It's nice to have so much room.

Another important thing is we have two cats in our family now. Geno got to name them and he picked Boo and Bud. They can go outside during the day, but they are always inside at night. We got Boo and Bud as kittens when they were surrendered to the humane society last Christmas in a cooler without a top. Taj brought them home.

Lost didn't like them in the beginning.

The cats have never understood that he's a dog. They try to do everything he does and curl up with him when he's sleeping. They always want Lost to play. But it turns out you *can* teach an old dog new tricks. He stopped barking at the kittens and now that they're grown-up, he looks out for them like he's their dad. If Boo and Bud aren't in the house at night, Lost paces by the door until we let him go find his cats. He's getting older and Geno says "he's got clouds in his eyes." But he still understands that his job is to protect the property, and he barks at anything that moves. Except Boo and Bud. He never barks at them.

In our new place we are all learning to play pool, because the pool table stayed. The McKerns also left the

TVs because they wanted to get "updated electronics" in Arizona, which is where their new second house is. But I don't watch TV very much. I still like to sit outside under the awning on the deck. I don't do that to get good internet because we have a strong signal all over the house. I go there to listen to the wind come up off the ocean and whistle across the sand dunes and the river.

I go out there to watch the Siuslaw.

I write to Button and I let her know what's going on. It turns out that you *can* have a friend who doesn't live in your town, it just takes some work to stay close.

The movers the McKerns hired forgot to take the wine that was in the special refrigerator in the basement. It was on the list, so that was a big mistake. When we told them, they got a price to have it all packed and shipped, but they decided it wasn't worth it. They asked us to donate the bottles somewhere in town so they could take a write-off, which is a way they can save money on taxes. Mom and Taj took pictures of all the labels on the bottles, and gave them to the library for their big auction, which is a once-a-year fundraiser. Someone from Palo Alto who just got a second house here on Shoreline Drive bought every bottle. Mrs. Hunt was so happy, because the library lost part of their funding in the new city budget. So some people are drinking fancy wine, and other people are reading new books.

Taj put an alarm on the McKerns' wine cooler, because

that wasn't auctioned off. He gets an alert if the temperature isn't right. He uses it as a veterinary fridge. Some of the medicine for the animals he takes care of has to be kept cold to work right. And putting food or anything to drink next to medicine isn't hygienic. Taj has taught me about all of that. You could almost say I'm a veterinarian's assistant. I have learned a lot.

We have a permit from the state of Oregon to foster wild animals, and that's what we use the boathouse for. We've had a big brown bat, a long-tailed weasel, and so many baby chipmunks and Douglas squirrels, which probably feels all wrong to Lost.

I helped rehabilitate an owl with a broken wing, and a bald eagle that was shot, which is a crime. They both were released back into the wild. Taj gives me the feeling that I'm not in the way and I can really help. He told me that he'd never met someone who was so good with birds, which means a lot because he doesn't exaggerate about stuff.

We also fostered two fledgling green herons after the tree holding their nest got cut down. I named them Randy and Tim. One of the herons had a fractured leg bone. Taj made a splint and we had to keep the two siblings apart while it healed. When we reunited them, it was a great day. I took a Polaroid picture. Now whenever I see a green heron in the wetlands, I think it might be Randy or Tim.

One of the best things about how we live now is that

Geno and I go out with Taj on weekend rescues. We've moved stranded sea turtles, and made so many house calls to people who have found injured wildlife. Jose comes with us a lot of the time too. I'm not afraid to be by the ocean anymore, especially when we're all together.

Mom stopped working at Curly's Seafood over a year ago. She went back to Lane Community College and finished her degree to be a registered nurse. But she's going to take more classes, so she can become a physician's assistant. They get to do even more important things and the hospital here needs help because we are such a small town.

She and Taj have a lot in common because she takes care of people and he takes care of animals.

I'm happy about how things turned out, but it wasn't all bad when we lived in the boathouse. There is a part of me that will always miss being in that place, even with doorknobs that fell off and a roof that leaked in the worst kitchen in the world.

In the boathouse, things were always breaking, but maybe we were what got repaired.

Do stepparents step up to help?

Do they step in?

Do they watch out so you don't take the wrong step?

We are Taj's stepchildren.

I looked up the word *stepchild*, and it has been around for more than a thousand years. Some people say it comes from one of the first Old English words for *orphan*. But I also read that it comes from a word that meant someone was robbed of something. If a kid had lost a parent, a stepparent was the replacement.

You don't have to lose a parent like we did in The Accident.

Sometimes, which is the case for my friend Ava Berger, who I'm a lot closer to since Button left, you get a stepmom but you keep your other mom. It's a bonus situation.

Damian Dewey has a stepdad who shares his collection of Star Wars memorabilia. Damian says they spend hours together looking for that stuff.

It was Geno who first got rid of the word *stepfather*. He was introducing Mom and Taj to a kid he met at the beach, and he said, "These are my parents."

Before, it had been his mom and his stepdad.

I heard him, and I felt something inside me move. In a good way.

I knew he was right.

Taj didn't save us. He says we saved him.

He told us he thought he'd waited too long to have kids and he'd never met the right person. He was there for his parents when they were sick and he missed his "window of opportunity."

But now he says he has everything he'd ever hoped for. Or dreamed about.

It's hard to be mad at someone who has so much love to give.

My Polaroid camera from Valerie changed the color of things. It made everything blurry on the edges. It showed the world in a different way. But that's true of all pictures. They are only capturing certain things. That's why it's sometimes good to close your eyes and make the picture yourself.

Valerie says that happened when she started to have trouble seeing. She had to rely on other ways of understanding the world, but important stuff is in your memory and it stays with you.

You draw a picture in your mind every time you remember.

Maybe the more it means to you, the stronger the picture becomes.

You can't share what that feels like.

It belongs to only you.

It was because of Lost that I was down at the river and saw dolphins. And when I wanted to know more, I went to the library on a Saturday with my little brother. And because I lost track of time when I was reading books, Geno wandered into the Bromley Room. He tried to look interested in a presentation because he wanted cookies and a juice box. That's why he ended up taking the brochure for the free services at the humane society. And because I went to the free clinic looking for help for Lost's bad breath, we met Taj.

Finding Lost changed everything.

The dolphins were never going to come visit me every day or be my pets. They are wild animals that have a life with other marine mammals. I saw one that was born special and was pink. And even if I never see her again, I know she's out there.

That helps me feel strong inside.

If you're lucky, you get good people in your life like Janice Hunt and Old Valerie Crowley.

You get a dog as loyal as Lost.

You get a friend as important as Button.

You get a second dad who wants to join your family and love you.

I had a great father.

I'm here because he once was.

And for me, that's enough.

AUTHOR'S NOTE

This book was inspired by Kyle and Amber Novelli, who died in 2020 when their crabbing boat sunk in the Siuslaw River after it hit the south jetty, just before two a.m. That morning, waves in the Pacific Ocean were as high as ten feet near the mouth of the river. When I read about the Novellis' passion for their seafood business, I couldn't stop thinking of the special people who work hard every day enriching life in small town communities. This story comes from my admiration for them.

ACKNOWLEDGMENTS

As always, my first thank-you goes to my publisher and editor, Lauri Hornik. She and my agent, Amy Berkower, make it all possible with their insight, guidance, and affection.

I'm equally fortunate to have Jen Loja, President of Penguin Young Readers, as a friend and great supporter of my work. The whole PYR team deserves thanks and credit for making it happen, especially: Regina Castillo, Kenny Young, Jayne Ziemba, Vanessa Robles, Maya Tatsukawa, Jessica Jenkins, Sarah Jospitre, Carmela Iaria, Trevor Ingerson, Venessa Carson, Summer Ogata, Alex Garber, Lauren Festa, Christina Colangelo, Shanta Newlin, Lizzie Goodell, Emily Romero, Becky Green, and Abby Fritz.

At Writers House, I'm so very lucky to work with Tom Ishizuka and Celeste Montano.

I'm blessed with people in my life who read early drafts and help me wrestle ideas to the ground. On this book that was Katie Kleinsasser, Phyllis Grann, Teri Mason, Alisa Allen, Ginger Moshofsky, and Calvin Sloan.

I love the cover of *Finding Lost*, and the talented Francesco Buongiorni is responsible.

And from my days as a kid growing up in Oregon–it was all better because of Amy Addison Rudolf, Chrisanne Briot Mehl, Kathy Golden Schwartz, Carroll Dizney Schwartz, Nancy Moshofsky Henderson, Annie Holland, Bob Glass, Mark Murphy, Chris Overton, Greg Ausland, Pierre Van Rysselberghe, Sara Bingham, Sue Cross, Greg Rose, Daphne Ruff, Janis McGhee Hubbard, Bonnie and John Marineau, Leah Grotzinger, Carl Christoferson, Teri Byrd, Monte Matthews, Chris Jaeger, Rod MacKinnon, and Paul Terry and Hank Flake (both gone but never forgotten).

My final debt of gratitude goes to Gary A. Rosen.